DATE DUE

Demco

Published by
Harmony Ink Press
5032 Capital Circle SW
Suite 2, PMB# 279
Tallahassee, FL 32305-7886
USA
publisher@harmonyinkpress.com
http://harmonyinkpress.com

Every Inferno
© 2014 Johanna Parkhurst.

Cover Art
© 2014 Reese Dante.
http://www.reesedante.com
Cover content is for illustrative purposes only
and any person depicted on the cover is a model.

ISBN: 978-1-62798-798-1
Library ISBN: 978-1-62798-800-1
Digital ISBN: 978-1-62798-799-8

Printed in the United States of America
First Edition
July 2014

Library Edition
October 2014

For Riley, who loved JJ and McKinley first
and kept me believing in them.
You are a true Dr. Ben.

And with huge appreciation for all
the amazing folks at Harmony Ink Press.
Dunham, there aren't enough italics,
junk words, or epithets in the
English language to express my thanks.

CHAPTER 1

A SMELL that wasn't there before filled the bathroom.

JJ drew in a deep breath, trying to match the scent to anything that might already exist in his short memory. It was a difficult scent to describe: like pine trees, but not the real ones in his backyard. More like the smell of the stuff his father used to clean the kitchen floor.

He tried to push off the sudden sense of apprehension that filled him; who cared if someone else had also come into the restroom? This was his town, the tiny world he had spent his entire five years in, and there was a good chance he knew whoever else had just joined him.

Even if he didn't know anyone who went around smelling like pine trees.

JJ took a few breaths and flushed the toilet, eager to get back to the movie and his parents.

As he shoved the door of the stall open, though, the scent grew stronger. The person who had brought the scent in with him—a man—was facing the wall across the room. He was wearing a backpack and hugging his arms to his chest.

"I did it... I did it," the man whispered. "I finally did it."

JJ moved to the sinks, more eager than ever to return to the comforting gaze of his mother. But the noise of his sneakers against the tile alerted the man to JJ's presence, and now the stranger was turning around to face him.

It was the oddest sensation to only be able to see certain details of a person: blue jeans, a red long-sleeve shirt. And then a detail so clear it almost seemed to be the only thing JJ could see: the outline of a long and winding paintbrush, tattooed on the man's hand, snaking down from just below his thumb to where it disappeared beneath the cuff of his shirt.

But nothing else. No other details were there. The man was faceless. The color of hair was... what was it? It was as if it had never been there.

Then JJ could see nothing, and all he could hear was the man shouting. Something about how JJ shouldn't be there, and he couldn't know, and it wasn't time yet....

The pain began then. Horrible, burning, pain, and JJ knew he was screaming, but he couldn't hear himself over the roaring in his ears. He needed to find the door, the door, where was the door—

JACOB JASPER Jones woke up sweating, twisted into a trap of sheets and blankets. He frantically cast his eyes around the walls of his bedroom, looking for anything that would remind him he was *not* in that restroom again. There was the Modest Mouse poster, his bookshelf, the old dresser that had once belonged to his aunt—yes, he was safe.

Safe from *what?* Or *who?*

JJ quietly wrestled with the covers, thankful that he wasn't a screamer and didn't seem to have woken Aunt Maggie up. If it was up to JJ, Maggie would never know that JJ was having dreams about that day again.

They'd started about a month ago. Before then JJ had never dreamed anything specific about the fire. The nightmares were always vague and mushy, filled with flames and noise and not much else.

Not like this dream. This dream was clear and specific and so real it was as though JJ was reenacting every detail from that day. Right up until the end, when the faceless man turned and everything went black.

It was so vivid that JJ was starting to think it might be more than just a dream. That it might be a memory.

JJ'd never remembered much from that day. In fact, when the police had questioned him years earlier, he hadn't really been able to tell them anything. They'd blamed "psychological trauma" and wondered if JJ had possibly witnessed the setting of the second fire in the restroom, or if he'd just been unlucky enough to be in a stall when it happened.

Now JJ couldn't decide if this dream was his memory coming back or his mind playing sick tricks on him.

He lowered himself down to peer under the mattress of the lower bunk bed and pull out the bottle of cheap whiskey that Lewis had gotten some college student to buy for them a few weeks ago. Midway through his third swig, JJ finally felt a sense of calm taking over his body, and he wondered, not for the first time, what he should do. He could go to the police, tell them that maybe he had some new information—only what new information did he really have? That he was dreaming of a faceless person with a tattoo?

Another swig. The *tattoo*. JJ knew it might be the most important part of the dream. It was so clear in his mind.

But what if it wasn't a memory? What if it was just something JJ's head was creating? Did people go to the police about dreams?

The calm that the whiskey had brought on was starting to fade, and JJ decided to take a walk. He knew just where he needed to go.

JJ PEERED at the walls of the police station, reading the signs to keep his attention focused on something other than his stomach, which was feeling the effects of the whiskey. He hoped that by keeping his concentration on the signs, he might be able to keep his dinner where it was.

It was either there or on the bench next to him. Handcuffed as JJ was, there didn't appear to be many other places it could go.

He was starting to think he should have decided to just come to the police about the dream. Because at least then he'd be here of his own free will.

"Jacob Jones?" The woman above him definitely sounded irritated. JJ couldn't really blame her. After all, there had to be more exciting cases out there than dealing with a fifteen-year-old juvenile delinquent.

"JJ."

"Whatever. Your aunt's waiting for you in the hallway." She uncuffed him from the bench, and JJ unconsciously rubbed his hands around his sore wrists. So handcuffs really were as annoying as they looked in the movies.

In the hallway stood Aunt Maggie, looking every bit as irritated as the cop. She barely made eye contact with JJ before she turned and swept out of the station. JJ followed, not sure exactly how low to hang his head. He felt a little guilty, but not all that much—after all, what he had done was barely a crime. So he'd trespassed when he'd climbed on top of the movie theater. Big deal. He hadn't broken anything, or coveted, or violated any of the other commandments. No harm, no foul.

Still, he had a feeling that wasn't what Aunt Maggie wanted to hear. He tried to look at least a little contrite.

They were in the car before she spoke to him. "You. Are. In. Big. Trouble."

Duh. He'd been arrested. Even if Aunt Maggie hadn't been upset, which obviously wasn't turning out to be the case, JJ was pretty sure the arrest itself was going to be an issue.

"Arrested. For trespassing. That will go on your record. Unless I can find some saintlike lawyer to deal with you and your incessant need to give me an early heart attack. Not to mention that you snuck out of the house at one o'clock in the morning. You are in *big trouble.*"

She didn't say anything the rest of the way home. After unlocking the door and letting them both inside, she stared at him for a few seconds in the dark kitchen before she spoke again.

"I am going to bed. You are too. When you wake up, you will immediately begin making this house sparkle. That's how clean it will be. Then we'll decide when, if ever, you will leave the house again."

Maggie stormed off to her bedroom and slammed the door.

JJ sighed and moved toward his room, wondering if he'd left anything in that whiskey bottle.

HE WAS awake early the next day, with only twinges of a hangover. He hadn't been drunk enough to do major damage. JJ moved toward the shower and wondered how seriously he should take Maggie's cleaning directive.

It was a toss-up, really. Aunt Maggie's bark was often worse than her bite, and she might not be so angry after a good night's sleep. Maybe JJ could get away with just making her breakfast.

You were arrested, moron, he reminded himself. This probably wasn't going to go over quite as easily as the time he'd put the dead frogs from the science lab all over the tables in the cafeteria. At least he'd been able to write that off as a political protest.

JJ decided to make breakfast while he was cleaning the kitchen. Maybe looking like he was trying to apologize would somehow get him out of the rest of the job.

Breakfast was definitely the easiest meal to make. JJ liked cooking. He enjoyed taking random ingredients and forming them into something. He liked eating, and it was fun experimenting with different flavors to see what odd combinations tasted good.

This morning he thought he'd try orange-banana waffles. He swept up the kitchen while the batter was sitting and did the dishes as his eggs cooked and the bacon hissed in the pan. He had a plate sitting out for Maggie and was cutting up melon for a fruit salad when she came in.

"Making amends? Or just trying to get out of the rest of the cleaning?" she asked dryly.

JJ opened his mouth to respond, but she cut him off quickly. "Honestly, it smells so good I don't really care. Good diversion, kid." She settled into her seat and poured syrup onto her waffles. "Nice flavor," she said after the first bite. "Very interesting."

JJ brought the fruit he was cutting over to the table and sat down next to her. He knew he should say something, and he thought it should probably begin with "I'm sorry."

"I'm sorry," he said.

Maggie shook her head. "No you're not."

JJ pretended to concentrate on the melon. "I'm sorry you're pissed. I'm sorry all I do is piss you off."

"You often do." Maggie took a sip of juice. "We both know you're only apologizing right now because it's what your dad would have told you to do. We both know he didn't quite make it to all the lessons of right and wrong, or you wouldn't have done what you did last night."

JJ scowled a little. Anyone else saying that about his dad would already have a bruise somewhere, but Maggie played by different rules. JJ's dad had been her brother.

"I'm here to tell you that your father would be very disappointed, Jacob Jasper."

JJ turned away. "That's a low blow, Aunt Mag. I didn't do anything that bad last night. I just wanted to go to the top of the theater. I just wanted to…." He stopped. What had he been trying to do? He wasn't sure. All he knew was that somewhere in the buzzy haze of the whiskey, JJ had thought visiting the theater would give him a better idea of what to do about that stupid dream.

He was just sitting there—not hurting anyone—when someone had come up behind him. Then the handcuffs had come out.

Maggie sighed and took a bite of egg. "Well cooked." She swallowed. "Look, hon, I know that you trespassing on the top of the theater wasn't exactly a coincidence. I get that, I really do. I realize that you were probably not out to cause trouble when you climbed up there last night. The problem, JJ, is that you usually aren't… but trouble comes anyway. We're going to have to find a lawyer. There will be consequences for this."

JJ sliced into an orange. "I know."

"JJ, I love you. So much. But you can't ride on the coattails of your pain your whole life. Plenty of kids have been through worse. Plenty of kids are going through worse. Plenty of kids are not getting their aunts called to police stations at two a.m. because they can't control their own behaviors. Do you know what Darryl will say when she hears about this? Do you know how long it will be before I'll be able to get you and Penny together again?"

Anger cut through JJ's system. "She's my sister, Maggie!"

"And she's my niece. But when Darryl adopted her, I gave up my rights to play either card. And I made a deal with Darryl that I'd tell her about any trouble you got into. You know I'm going to have to tell Darryl about this, and you know Darryl isn't going to like it. JJ, she kept Penny away for a month that time you started a food fight in eighth grade. How do you think she'll respond to you getting arrested for trespassing?"

"God, I hate her!" JJ snarled the words as he slammed the knife through the orange, and Maggie gasped.

"JJ?"

Looking down, JJ saw blood splashing through the bowl of Maggie's fruit salad. Suddenly he felt very light-headed, and he noticed more blood gushing from a cut in the side of his left hand before he felt the wave of pain there. "I missed the orange," he mumbled.

Maggie pulled him out of his chair, wrapping his hand in a dish towel that immediately stained pink. "Let's go!" she urged.

IT DIDN'T take JJ long to figure out that it wasn't a bad idea to be pouring blood out of your system when you walked into an emergency room. Judging by the amount of people there, they might have been waiting all day—but the admitting nurse took one look at the bright red towel wrapped around JJ's hand and the glazed expression in his eyes and sent them to a room immediately.

It wasn't really a room, of course. More like a bunch of beds lined up next to each other. JJ lay down on the bed the nurse indicated, and she started asking Maggie a million questions about JJ's allergies and how he'd cut himself. Then there was a whole lot of silent waiting while Maggie paced and JJ tried not to stare at his hand.

The doctor who finally approached them wasn't young. JJ thought he was probably in his early forties, right around the age JJ's father would have been. He was tall, with dark blond hair and a nose that was a little bigger than the rest of his face. He was smiling widely. And even though he didn't look anything like Jasper Jones, JJ felt the twinge of his father's absence that sometimes crept up on him.

"Hello! I'm Dr. Ben. I hear this one's a gusher!" Dr. Ben slowly unwrapped the towel from JJ's hand and sucked in his breath a little. "Not wide, but deep. How did you do this?"

JJ still felt woozy, and he wondered briefly if this was just another dream. "I was making breakfast. I missed the orange."

The doctor shook his head. "Did you lay in the knife after you missed? It looks like you just missed a vein here. Lucky kid." He removed the towel and replaced it with a large bandage. "No worries, though. I've seen worse. We'll stitch you right up and have you back at the fruit in no time."

Maggie sighed with relief. "I swear, JJ, I'm getting a whole lot closer to that heart attack I was talking about last night." JJ squirmed, not sure how to respond to that, but the doctor laughed.

"Ma'am, you look paler than he does. Might I suggest a little coffee from the cafeteria while I stitch him up? I'm not sure it will do your heart good to watch the process."

Maggie nodded eagerly. "Will you be okay, JJ?"

JJ couldn't imagine anything better than her leaving. "Get some coffee, Aunt Mags. I'll be fine."

Maggie left, and JJ settled back against the pillow while the doctor found some kind of kit. He gave JJ a shot, and then JJ could hardly feel his hand. It felt like an out-of-body experience as he watched the doctor move the needle in and out of his skin like it was a quilt the guy was working on.

"You hurt yourself a lot?" Dr. Ben asked.

"Huh?"

"I wondered if you do things like this a lot. You seem to have a pretty high pain threshold."

JJ winced. He'd heard that before. Ten years before, actually. "I've never cut myself like that before. I just… I almost didn't feel it all that much." JJ closed his eyes and leaned back against the bed, trying not to think about the last doctor who had said those words, as he had examined the burns tracing across the back of JJ's small legs.

"Everything okay?" Dr. Ben asked. JJ figured he'd noticed the wince.

"Course."

"Just let me know if you start to feel anything."

JJ opened one eye. "Sure. So, why are you called Dr. Ben, anyway? That doesn't sound very professional."

Dr. Ben chuckled. "I'm a pediatrician. I'm just doing a stint in the ER right now to help out. My real last name is Peragena, and most kids have problems with that."

"Whatever."

"Yep. It works. So, is your aunt gonna make it? She looked pretty white."

JJ sighed. "I'm not the easiest person to live with. She's a wedding photographer though, so I think she deals with worse at work." JJ considered that for a minute. Aunt Mags never got a break. Demanding brides all day, a juvenile delinquent at home....

"You live with her?"

"Yeah." JJ hoped Dr. Ben wouldn't ask where his parents were. It was always an awkward question, because JJ hated to answer it. Most of the time he stayed silent while the other person waited for a response. He and a stubborn shrink had once stared each other down for ten minutes over that question. Finally the shrink gave up.

Dr. Ben didn't say anything, though. He finished up the stitches and wrapped gauze around JJ's hand before giving him a quick lecture about the proper care of suture wounds. Aunt Maggie came back just as he was finishing up.

"I think Frankenstein here will be fine," Dr. Ben told her. "I'm going to have him rest here for a bit, though, just to make sure we don't need to add more blood to his system. That work for you, Frank?"

JJ rolled his eyes. Sometimes when adults were trying to be funny they just ended up sounding so... stupid. "Sure, Dr. Ben."

JJ closed his eyes again. At least he'd have a break before Maggie started yelling at him again.

"...It's never been easy, but this last year or so has been particularly difficult. He isn't a bad kid, he isn't. He's just always into something! There was the frog incident, and he and his friends stole all of the hand sanitizer out of the front office at school, and then I caught him smoking cigarettes in the backyard. I know he's drinking; I smell it on him from time to time. I practically have to lock him in the house these days. Last night I think he's gone to bed, and the next thing I know he's at the police station. I'm at my wit's end. My brother would kill me if he knew what I was doing to his kid."

JJ rubbed his eyes groggily. He was on the bed at the hospital, and he had a little more feeling back in his sore hand. He could actually feel it throb now. How long had he been asleep? And was that Maggie talking about him?

"I'm sorry to unload like this, doctor, but clearly I'm reaching the level of needing medical help. The school has tried, but their psychologist can't even get JJ to talk to her. They just keep telling me I'm doing the right thing to keep on him at home, and they'll keep on him at school. They keep telling me he'll 'straighten out' eventually. I don't even know what that means anymore."

JJ rolled his eyes. The school psychologist was an idiot, just like all the other shrinks Maggie had made him see over the years. This one had even tried to get to him draw pictures. What was he, six?

"Now the whole thing is drawing blood. We were arguing this morning about what he's doing to his relationship with his sister, and he got angry and distracted and nearly took his hand off! I swear to you, my brother is rolling over in his grave right now."

Yeah, JJ had heard that before—he was a huge disappointment, and his parents would be horrified if they could see all the poor choices he was making… blah blah blah. He'd already heard it from Maggie at breakfast, and he'd been hearing it from people his whole life. Still, JJ couldn't help but notice that a lump the size of a cherry rose into his throat at the phrase "rolling over in his grave."

"Ms. Dunsmore, I think you're being too hard on yourself. You're doing the best you can. How long have you been JJ's legal guardian?"

"They died when he was five. I've had JJ since he was six… nine years, I guess."

"Nine years is amazing! In nine years he's a relatively normal teenage boy. You think you're the first woman to have a troublemaking fifteen-year-old in her house?"

"He isn't normal, though. He's so angry, Dr. Ben. I see it. I see it in the way he looks at me when he's done something wrong. Like the world owes him anyway, and this is just his way of trying to even the score. Not with me, I don't think… with God."

Well, that was just dumb. There sure was somebody JJ would love to settle a score with. But it wasn't God.

"Ms. Dunsmore, do you mind if I ask how JJ's parents died?"

The lump welled up in JJ's throat again. If this had been his conversation, here the room would have gone completely silent. But Aunt Maggie wasn't him.

"They were killed in the Bijou Street Theater fire, Dr. Ben. JJ was with them. He was very lucky and managed to make it out alive."

A deep, heavy silence—the kind that JJ would normally have created—fell. Only this time it was apparently being created by Dr. Ben.

"Dr. Ben? Are you all right?"

It sounded like Dr. Ben was deeply clearing his throat. "I'm fine, Ms. Dunsmore. Just a little caught off guard."

"You're sure you're okay?"

"I am; I'm fine. My daughter passed away in that fire. I just haven't heard anyone mention it in quite some time."

"Oh!" JJ could hear Maggie's sharp intake of breath. "I'm so sorry. I sometimes wish we kept more distance from it as well. We really never have, though. It's mentioned almost every day at our house. I'm sorry I brought it up."

"No, no. It's fine. Maybe it's good for JJ that it's not a taboo subject in your household."

"Maybe. Sometimes I wonder if we talk about it entirely too much. It's not something we can just put in the backs of our minds, though. Not with JJ's legs."

Even hidden behind the curtain, JJ squirmed uncomfortably as Dr. Ben asked his next question: "JJ's legs?"

"Yes. He was in the theater's restroom that day. He made it out alive, but his legs caught on fire. He has horrendous scar tissue up and down his calves."

No one spoke for a few moments after that, and JJ thought they had walked away from the curtain, when he suddenly heard Dr. Ben's voice again.

"Your nephew—he was the boy who was rescued from the restroom that day?"

"Yes. You remember that? I mean, I suppose he was all over the Moreville newspapers for a while. Still, that was so long ago."

"I… no, I didn't recall the newspaper articles. I was the man who pulled him out."

JJ sat up quickly, looking for his clothes. He didn't need a theater roof to figure out whether his dreams were real; the person who could help him figure it out was three feet away!

But Dr. Ben was already saying, "Ma'am, I'm sorry, I have to run… other patients…."

By the time JJ got the curtain open, only Maggie was standing there. She looked at JJ with wide eyes. "I guess you heard that, huh?"

JJ frowned. He had a bad feeling he wasn't going to see Dr. Ben again anytime soon. He knew from experience you didn't go looking for things you were desperately trying to forget.

ON THE drive home, JJ half expected Maggie to cluck and fuss over his hand, but she didn't say much, except to ask if it still hurt. JJ said it just ached, mostly. They pulled into their driveway, and she announced that she didn't think it would be difficult for him to dust and tidy with one hand. When he felt better, he could do the bathrooms.

"And no leaving the house or using the Internet until I say otherwise. And I'm taking your cell phone. No texting or Facebooking or whatever else you do on there. Absolutely no contact with the outside world until I tell you that you are no longer a prisoner in this house." She went down to her basement office with some line about "feeling his presence above her," leaving JJ to stare around at the mess in the kitchen.

And to think.

JJ was a thinker. He was quiet. Teachers often complained that part of the reason he had the reputation he did in school, as a disrespectful slacker, was because he wouldn't talk. He frequently responded in monosyllables, and sometimes he was so deep in his own head when a teacher called on him that he just didn't answer at all. He wasn't trying to be a jerk. He just liked it better in his head than anywhere else.

Right now, though, his head was buzzing, and he was having trouble keeping up with it. *Dr. Ben had been in the restroom with him at the movie theater that day.* Just thinking about it made JJ so anxious that he actually picked up the duster and attacked Grandma's old kitchen hutch.

When the dreams had first started, JJ had researched everything he could find that might tell him whether or not the dream was real. He'd read every newspaper and police report he could get his hands on. He knew that the tattoo he was seeing in his dream had never been brought up—at least not publicly—in connection with the case. He knew that almost every person killed had been in Theater Three, because the fire exit to that theater had been blocked. He knew that if Dr. Ben's daughter had died, she must have been in that theater, along with JJ's parents. He knew that a second blaze had been set in the theater's restroom, and that someone had pulled him out of the fire in that restroom.

But he'd never known who had pulled him out. In the chaos of the fire, the man who had rescued JJ had never been identified by the media, and he'd never come forward to accept public congratulations for saving a five-year-old from certain death.

JJ knew that if Dr. Ben had been the one to pull him out of the bathroom, he might be the only one who could confirm if anything in JJ's dream was real.

Like the tattoo.

JJ was tempted to slice into his other hand and send himself back to the hospital. At least with two damaged hands he wouldn't be expected to do schoolwork. But that would hurt, a lot, and JJ hadn't loved all the blood from his first accident of the day. Anyway, he could make sure he found a way to talk to Dr. Ben. The hospital was only a few blocks away from his high school.

If Maggie thought JJ was out to settle a score with God, she really didn't know him at all. The only score JJ had was with the person who had killed his parents. The person who had left JJ on fire, dying, in a restroom. The person who had eluded the police for almost ten years. That was the person JJ had a score to settle with.

And Dr. Ben might be just the person to help him do that.

CHAPTER 2

THE NEXT day was Monday—school. JJ claimed his hand hurt too much for him to go, but Aunt Maggie was having none of that. She just reminded him that she'd signed the school's waiver to give him Tylenol if he needed it and said, "If it becomes unlivable, you can wait in the nurse's office until I can come pick you up."

"Infections cause death within a few hours, you know," JJ called as he left the house. He had no idea if that was true, but it sounded good.

Lewis was at the corner where they usually met, playing something on a brand-new PSP. Lewis had a lot of money. His father was some kind of stock trader, and his mother was one of the best-known lawyers in their town. Lewis spent a lot of time trying to "wreck their good names," as he put it. JJ was sure that if anyone was angry at God, it was Lewis. Lewis wanted to be a video-game programmer, and his father wanted him to be the next football star of Warren Watkins High School. But they didn't talk about that sort of thing much. JJ just took the liquor that Lewis got for him and let Lewis talk him into things like The Great Frogfest, as they liked to call it.

Lewis glanced down at JJ's hand. "What did ya do?"

JJ knew Lewis wouldn't really care unless the story involved JJ doing something that caused a lot of problems or got a lot of attention.

"I just cut it making breakfast."

"Oh. Boring."

"Yup."

They walked to school, Lewis playing on his PSP and JJ lost in his head the whole way. That was how it usually went.

SCHOOL SURE wasn't motivating JJ to do what his shrink told him and become more "outgoing." As he sat through first period—Geometry—JJ remembered why it would have been so convenient to use his hand as an excuse to miss this class. Math sucked at the best of times, but at this hour of the day, it almost fell into the category of pure torture. JJ spent the period staring out the window and wondering if Dr. Ben would be working that afternoon.

At least Creative Writing was next. That was JJ's favorite class; it was the only elective he'd actually looked forward to when he was signing up for it. So far he hadn't been disappointed. They wrote in journals most of the time and read "model writing" or each other's writing. That was the only part JJ didn't like: reading his writing aloud, or "workshopping," as Ms. Lyle called it. The rest of the class was supposed to critique it for areas of improvement; JJ wasn't having any of that.

He thought Ms. Lyle would throw him out of her class when he first refused to show his writing to the rest of the room, but she'd just shrugged.

"Since it's on the syllabus for the course, I'm going to have to dock you points," she told him. "But if you don't mind that, I sure won't take the trouble to lose my temper over it." JJ spent the workshop portions of the class in silence, critiquing other people's writing in his head but refusing to say anything. Sometimes Ms. Lyle would raise her eyebrows at him, as though she expected him to, and JJ always just raised his right back. It hadn't thrown her off yet.

Today, though, they were writing for most of the class and then reading some examples of strong dialogue. Good. JJ eased into a desk and pulled his black marbled composition book out from between his other books.

"Good Lord!" exclaimed Ms. Lyle, eyeing his injured hand. "What happened?"

JJ shrugged, pulling a pencil out of his pocket and flipping the book open to write. Ms. Lyle just winced at the sight of the bandage wrapped around his skin and flitted across the room to start taking attendance. JJ smiled. This was why he loved Creative Writing and why Ms. Lyle was his favorite teacher. Other teachers were instantly pissed off by JJ's nonresponses. They added other adjectives to the list they had running about him in their heads. Words like "passive-aggressive," "depressed," "defiant." Then they either held his silence against him for the rest of the class, week, or year, or they made it a goal to get him to speak by asking him as many questions as possible. That always led to more monosyllabic or non-answers from JJ, which led to more mental adjectives stacked against him in their heads. It was a vicious cycle.

But Ms. Lyle never perpetuated it. JJ was pretty sure the only thing he could ever do to get Ms. Lyle to start stacking adjectives against him would be to stop writing—which JJ wasn't doing anytime soon. He had signed up for this class to write. All class period, if possible.

Today he was working on a story about Detective Morris Finch. Detective Finch was a character JJ had been writing about since the fifth grade. He was an arson investigator. He always caught the criminal.

JJ didn't tell too many people about Detective Finch. A school psychologist in junior high had gotten hold of one of his stories once and made a big deal about how the stories showed that JJ had a lot of "repressed anger" about the person behind the Bijou fire not being caught.

That was exactly what JJ had been trying not to talk about as they'd sat in his office at least two days a week for the month before that.

Ms. Lyle could read Detective Finch, though. She probably knew about JJ's history in Moreville's most notorious fire, but she never mentioned it. For her, Detective Finch was just another character, another story, to grade JJ on. So far she seemed to like him. She said JJ's plots were well paced, and she thought the character was strong. (JJ was glad about that; if you couldn't get a strong character after five years, what hope did you have?) She just wanted him to work on Finch's voice. She kept commenting that it was a little too shallow and not interesting enough.

So JJ worked on Finch's voice as he went over the last part of the story he had just written, pulling out a comma here and there and changing lots of words. Finding the exact word, JJ thought, was somehow both the most exciting and most annoying challenge with writing. JJ just couldn't quite nail down what kind of vocabulary Detective Finch would use.

He could work on that, though. At least the plot was continuing to come together. Currently Detective Finch was on the trail of a corporate executive who had a lot to gain monetarily from the Alabastor Restaurant fire. JJ already knew exactly who the criminal was going to be—and it wasn't the restaurant executive.

"Journals... twenty minutes!" Ms. Lyle called. JJ settled back into the seat, happy to live in a world that wasn't his own for a while.

Six other excruciatingly long periods and one disgusting lunch later, JJ met Lewis on the north side of the high school. Lewis pulled a pack of cigarettes out of his back pocket and lit one up as they stepped off the high school property and onto the sidewalk.

"Smoke?" he offered.

JJ hesitated, then shook his head. He didn't love smoking, and when Maggie had caught him last week, she'd threatened to make him smoke a whole pack if she ever caught him doing it again. JJ thought she might actually go through with it, and he sure didn't like smoking *that* much.

It wasn't like he really enjoyed it at all, actually. It was just another thing he had started doing every now and then with Lewis because... well, he really didn't know why.

"Mike Keeball's having a party in that field that belongs to his dad this weekend. We should go. They're getting a keg," said Lewis.

That was good news, since JJ's bottle of whiskey was basically empty. Drinking took an edge off that JJ could never seem to shake otherwise. He'd gone to his first keg party with Lewis during their freshman year, and JJ still remembered it as being the first time he'd felt truly calm in years. There was always a spring within him that seemed to be wound way too tight. A drink loosened the spring better than anything else. After that night, JJ had figured out that there were lots of ways for a fourteen- or fifteen-year-old to get booze. Especially if you lived in a corner of Vermont that had more cows than people, and there wasn't a whole lot of entertainment around that didn't involve drinking or pot.

Pot wasn't really JJ's thing, though. It made him think even more than he usually did, and it usually wound the spring even tighter. Drinking definitely put JJ more in line with his goals.

"Course," JJ told Lewis.

At the corner of Southington Street and Main Street, JJ turned. "I have to run by the hospital. Wanna meet tomorrow morning?"

Lewis looked skeptical. "Weren't you just at the hospital?"

"Yeah. I need something they… want me to put on this cut. I didn't get it yesterday." JJ sure wasn't going to explain what he was planning to Lewis. Lewis was his friend, probably his best friend, but the fire wasn't something JJ talked about with anyone.

Except maybe another person who had been there.

"Sure, Jaje. Tomorrow. Call me if you want to go by the arcade tonight." Lewis pulled his PSP out of his pocket, and JJ listened to the tiny beeps and bells that quickly faded from the air as Lewis disappeared down the street.

Breathing a sigh of something—relief?—JJ started up the street to the hospital.

"I NEED to talk to Dr. Ben."

The woman at the Emergency Room front desk looked way too frazzled to remember seeing JJ there the day before. "Huh?" she practically yelled. "Charles, we need a gurney in here now! What do you need, son?"

JJ hated when people called him son. "Dr. Ben. I'd like to talk to Dr. Ben."

"There's no Dr. Ben here, son. Charlie!" she yelled over her shoulder.

Now JJ was getting frustrated. "Yes there is. He just stitched up my hand yesterday."

Another nurse looked up from a stack of paperwork. "Do you mean Dr. Peragena? He has an office in the pediatric wing of the hospital. He was just helping us out yesterday."

JJ thanked the helpful nurse, glared at the other one, and left the ER to find the Peds wing of the hospital.

It was bright and cheerful, with loud colors echoing in huge shapes off of every wall. JJ knew it shouldn't look familiar—it had probably changed multiple times since his stay here—but he recognized it all the same. He'd spent almost two weeks in a room somewhere in this wing, staring at the ceiling, not eating, not sleeping, barely talking to anyone.

His stomach churned as he moved through the halls, and JJ practically ran until he found the sign that read DR. BEN PERAGENA in gold letters.

The waiting room was noisy and filled with small children playing with toys and books. Parents were everywhere, trying to entertain and keep nerves calm. JJ ignored them and went straight to the desk.

"Could I please talk to Dr. Ben?"

This nurse was friendlier than the ER nurse. She smiled at JJ, and her glance stopped on his bandaged hand. "Do you need medical attention?"

JJ wasn't sure how to answer that. What would get him in to see Dr. Ben? Obviously the guy had a full schedule today. "Uh… kind of. He stitched up my hand in the ER yesterday. I just had a few questions about… my injury?" He wasn't sure if that last part came out as a question or a statement.

The nurse studied the computer in front of her. "He's very busy today. Is it something I can help with? Or another doctor in the building?"

JJ felt his heart sink a little. "I'd really like to talk to Dr. Ben," he mumbled. He knew he was doing everything his teachers couldn't stand. He was being monosyllabic and passive-aggressive and all those other adjectives they hated. He just didn't know how else to be.

The nurse's smile didn't waver, though. "Let me see if he can squeeze you in somewhere. Can I get your name?"

"Jacob Jones." The nurse walked through a closed door on her right, and JJ breathed heavily on the desk in front of him while he waited.

She reappeared a few minutes later. "He says he could squeeze you in if you'll wait a few minutes. How's that sound?"

JJ released a breath he didn't realize he'd been holding. "Sure." Then he sat down and concentrated on trying to find the hidden pictures in some old copy of *Highlights* magazine.

"SO, WHAT did you need to talk about, JJ?"

Dr. Ben had a nice office. A huge cherrywood desk like the one in Grandpa's old office, soft guest chairs, a couch, nice paintings on the walls. No family photos, JJ noticed. He'd never been in a doctor's office that didn't have a family photo somewhere in it.

JJ tried to mentally unwind the spring inside him. A drink would have helped. "I had a question for you."

"About your hand, right?" The slight smile at the right hand corner of Dr. Ben's mouth told JJ the doctor knew this had nothing to do with JJ's injury.

"Well… maybe not exactly. I didn't think your nurse would let me talk to you if I didn't say that."

Dr. Ben leaned forward. "What are you, JJ, fourteen?"

"Fifteen."

"Good. Then you'd probably also like to cut right to the chase. You're here about the Bijou Street Movie Theater fire, aren't you?"

The spring loosened a little. "Yeah. I heard you talking in the hospital. I heard what you said about… your daughter. About me."

Pain tightened Dr. Ben's face. "It's not a subject I enjoy discussing. I was surprised to hear about our… connection."

Suddenly JJ had to make sure Dr. Ben understood something. "So you know, Dr. Ben, I don't like talking about it either. I didn't blame you for not coming back to see me yesterday. I kind of won't talk about it most of the time. I mean, I drove a few psychologists crazy not talking about it. But I have to ask you something about it. I have to."

Now Dr. Ben nodded. "Ask away. There are some things, however, I won't answer."

JJ felt the respect he already had for Dr. Ben surge within him. This was someone he could talk to; he'd known it the minute Dr. Ben had responded to Aunt Maggie's comment about the fire. Dr. Ben understood. He wouldn't pry. He wouldn't try to figure out JJ, because he didn't need to.

"Listen, I've been having this dream lately. Pretty often, actually. And I think it's a memory from the day of the fire. Only I can't be sure—I'm worried it's something my mind, like, created. That it's not a memory at all. So I did some research."

Dr. Ben coughed in surprise. "I'm sorry?"

"Research. Trying to figure out if the details from that day match my dream. But the newspapers and stuff aren't helping. Only then I heard you say you were the guy who pulled me out of the bathroom. If anyone would know if my dream's real, you would. I thought—I don't know...." JJ couldn't figure out quite how to explain it. "I thought if you could tell me what you saw, maybe I'd know. Maybe I'd know if the dream is real."

Dr. Ben leaned forward and studied JJ. JJ tried not to squirm. "Do you mind if I ask, JJ, why it makes such a difference? Is it a psychological matter of some kind? Why does it make a difference if this dream is a memory or not?"

JJ frowned. "There's this detail in the dream. I think it might be important evidence—new evidence. I've never heard of it being in this case before. But I haven't said anything to anyone, because I don't know for sure that my mind didn't just make it up or something."

Dr. Ben nodded and leaned back. "Okay. You're hoping I can confirm this detail? That I saw it too?"

JJ frowned again. "I don't know. Maybe. Or maybe you'll be able to tell me that other things from the dream are real, and then I'll be able to figure out if that detail's real. I don't know." He shook his head. "I just have this weird feeling that you might be able to help me figure this whole thing out."

"Oh." Dr. Ben looked suddenly uncomfortable. "The thing is, JJ, that much of what I remember from that day is nothing more than the chaos that was surrounding us. I'm not sure how much help I'll really be."

JJ nodded. He was afraid Dr. Ben would say something like that.

Dr. Ben rapped his desk with his knuckles. "Let's try this. Would you mind telling me your dream first? Then I could simply confirm or deny, as they say, what I do remember. We can go from there."

JJ didn't think he was any more thrilled about sharing his dream than Dr. Ben was about listening to it. Well, at least he was finally spilling the story in a doctor's office. A dozen psychologists had begged for him to do that over the years. *Too bad they aren't here to see it*, JJ thought with some smugness.

He took a breath. "Okay. So, this part I remember; it's not from the dream. We were at the movies together, and I really had to pee. I didn't want my mom or dad to go with me. I was a pretty independent kid, even though I was only five, and I told them I was old enough to go by myself. And since this is a really safe town and all, they let me. I've never really remembered much after that... just faces and... some other stuff." JJ shuddered. "Then I started having this dream a while ago.

"It starts with me standing in the bathroom of the Bijou Street Movie Theater. I'm in the stall, and I smell something like pine. I push the door open, and there's this guy standing there. He's saying 'I did it!' over and over again.

"Then he turns around, but I can't see his face. And something else. Then everything kind of goes black, and I can't see anything anymore, but I know that everything around me catches on fire." JJ saw no need to share the part of the dream where the back of his calves were burning... no, smoldering. That part he knew for sure wasn't just a dream; that part had been locked in his memory, all too vividly, for years.

JJ's eyes were glued to Dr. Ben. What if Dr. Ben couldn't remember anything either? But Dr. Ben was staring at JJ like he'd seen a ghost. It felt like a long time before he cleared his throat and spoke.

"Are there any other details, JJ? Anything more specific? The detail you mentioned earlier?"

JJ's eyes widened a little bit. "Why? Did I say something you remember?"

Dr. Ben twisted his hands into each other, an anxious expression on his face. "I was coming down the hall, back from the lobby, toward Theater Three. I smelled smoke, and as I was nearing the restrooms, a man rushed by me. Then I saw smoke coming from under the restroom door, and I heard your screams. I opened up the door, saw you and the fire surrounding you, and I pulled you out.

"It was chaos by the time I got you out of that restroom. The alarms had gone off and there were people everywhere. We rolled you on the floor and got you out of the theater. I went looking for my daughter." Dr. Ben rushed through that sentence, and JJ worried for a second that he might stop talking entirely, but Dr. Ben continued: "JJ, when the police found out the fire had come from two places—both Theater Three and the restroom—they questioned me very intensively about the man I saw run from that area. They knew the arsonist had to be in that restroom at some point to start that second blaze. But the man went by me so quickly that I've never remembered any details about him, and apparently you haven't either. Until now. JJ, I think your dream is real. I think you did meet the arsonist in that bathroom that day, and I think whatever detail you're remembering is also likely to be real."

Dr. Ben leaned in closer to JJ, the intensity of his expression matching his voice. "You said you can't see his face, but you can see something else. So what is it you remember, JJ? What detail do you see in the dream?"

JJ didn't think he'd even been this focused on a conversation in his life. "It's his hand. There's something on his hand, Dr. Ben. It's a huge tattoo, and I could draw it, I can see it so clearly."

Dr. Ben looked a little white. He cleared his throat. "What's the tattoo of?"

"Well, that's the thing. I started to think my mind just invented that, because of what caused the fire. And *that* made me think maybe I never was in the bathroom with the guy at all. But if you saw him right before you rescued me, I *had* to have seen him, right? I must have. And I must have really seen the tattoo." JJ stopped to take a deep breath before he finally added, "It's a paintbrush. A long, skinny paintbrush."

Dr. Ben said nothing.

"Yup," JJ continued, "a paintbrush. It had to be him, Dr. Ben. Who else would use turpentine? And you saw him too. You saw him too."

Dr. Ben shook his head slowly. "A lot of people died that day, JJ." His murmured words hung in the air.

"Twenty-eight," JJ mumbled. The Bijou was a small movie theater; but it was also the only movie theater in Moreville. There had been three movies going on that afternoon, with each theater at least half-filled.

"Lots of people think the arsonist was specifically targeting Theater Three."

JJ nodded again. Someone had blocked the fire exit from the alley, so it took the people in the theater precious extra minutes to unwedge the exit door and get it open. The fire had been set in the front of the theater leading to that hallway, making it impossible for anyone inside to escape from that direction. The arsonist had almost certainly been targeting that theater.

"I would like nothing better than to find the person who murdered twenty-eight people that day, one of them being my daughter. JJ, will you allow me to call the police and let me give them this information?"

JJ nodded vigorously. "I'd really like that. I mean, I've been kinda wanting to call them for a while, but I was afraid it was all in my head, y'know? And I know they'll just add it to the file, and it might not mean anything yet... but maybe it could, later. It's something, right?"

Dr. Ben pulled a business card from the holder on his desk. "I'm going to give the police your contact information when I call, so you should probably expect them to be in touch. You'll need to get those stitches out in a little over a week. Call my office—we can compare notes of what we've heard from the investigators, and I'll get to see how you're healing."

JJ wasn't sure what to do next. He wasn't a hugger, or even a toucher, really. He finally settled on firmly shaking Dr. Ben's hand before he left.

He walked home slowly, replaying his conversation with Dr. Ben over and over in his mind. By the time he arrived at the doorstep of the house, the sky was already dark, and Maggie was waiting in the kitchen for him.

"It's a good thing you're taking your grounding seriously," she told him drily. "Also, the police called here looking for you. Anything you want to tell me, JJ?"

That conversation was going to take a while.

CHAPTER 3

JJ HAD been right a few nights ago—police stations were better when you were there by choice.

Maggie brought him over there the next evening, and they met with Detective Starrow. She was a fit middle-aged woman with bright red hair and dark eyes. JJ was glad she wasn't one of the original detectives who'd first opened the arson investigation ten years ago. If she had been, she would have remembered JJ from back then, and there probably would have been a lot of embarrassing sympathy and maybe even some hugging or something. But she'd only taken over the case five years ago when the original detective in charge had retired, so she just shook JJ's hand and said she was happy to meet him.

Since Dr. Ben's office was the first time in a long time that JJ had recounted the story of that day, and the first time he'd talked about the dream with anyone, it felt really awkward to spill it again in front of Maggie and a complete stranger. Maggie kept squeezing his hand, and JJ had to fight not to pull it away, since he didn't want Detective Starrow to think he was some kind of weirdo who didn't like to be touched.

Even if he actually was.

JJ finished up by explaining what the tattoo looked like, and Detective Starrow studied her notes intently. "JJ, it might sound strange, but I'd like to have you describe that tattoo to a sketch artist. I want to share it with tattoo shops around the area and see if we can get any leads there."

"Okay. So you don't think I'm making it up, then?"

The detective smiled slightly. "JJ, it wouldn't be *you* making it up, it would be your mind. And it's possible. The mind can be a funny thing. But the fact that the details of your dream match so closely to what Dr. Peragena remembers from that day is very intriguing. I'm glad the two of you talked and that you decided to tell us about the tattoo." She closed her notebook. "It's been a lot of years since we had any new information in this case. Frankly, I'll take what I can get. Wait here a second, all right? I'll see if our sketch artist is here today."

Maggie grabbed JJ's hand again. "JJ, I'm so proud of you. I know that wasn't easy for you."

JJ smiled slightly. "Uh, Maggie? Did you talk to Darryl yet? Am I going to get to see Penny this weekend?" Usually Darryl brought Penny over to Maggie's house every other Saturday or Sunday for a few hours. JJ liked it that way. Visits with Penny would have been ruined if he had to worry the whole time about running into Patrick.

Maggie sighed. "I was hoping you'd wait to ask that. I called her today and told her about what happened at the theater. She wasn't pleased, obviously. She wants to hold off on bringing Penny over until your arrest is cleared up."

"What? I thought you said that could take months!" JJ was appalled.

"I doubt it will take that long, JJ. I got in touch with a public defender who thinks he can clear the whole thing up in a few weeks."

JJ fumed silently, and Maggie went for his hand again. "JJ, we knew there was a strong chance this might happen. Darryl isn't your biggest fan on the best of days. Just keep your nose clean and do what you need to do while we clear this trespassing charge up. We'll get you and Penny back together."

JJ couldn't just let it go, though. Penny had been busy with some Girl Scout stuff for the past few weeks, so he already hadn't seen her for almost a month. And now it could be *another* month? Or even longer?

So after JJ had sat with some strange guy wearing huge glasses and described the paintbrush tattoo down to every shadow that he could see in his head, and after he and Maggie had gone home and were eating greasy Chinese food for dinner, he asked.

"I wanna call Penny." Okay, maybe it was more of a statement than a question.

Maggie took the last egg roll out of a carton. "Why? I told you what Darryl said, JJ."

JJ shrugged. "I know she said Penny couldn't come over. But maybe I could just talk to her."

Maggie frowned, and lines creased across her forehead. Whenever she did that, she looked so much like his father that JJ almost had to look away.

"Okay."

JJ stared. Had she said okay?

"On one condition."

There was always a condition.

"You have to have Darryl's permission to talk to Penny."

JJ deflated a little. He'd definitely been hoping that Penny would just magically be the person to answer the phone when JJ called. Still, Maggie hadn't said no. There was always a chance.

Maggie retreated to the basement, calling out something about thanking him for asking, and JJ dialed the number on the house phone, since Maggie still had his cell phone in lockup.

"Hello?" Crap. It was Patrick. Already things were going badly.

"Could I please talk to Darryl?"

"Who's this?" Patrick sounded suspicious. JJ thought about lying, but Patrick probably knew the sound of his voice, and lying wouldn't put him on very good footing if he finally got on the phone with Darryl.

"It's JJ. Listen, Patrick, I just need to talk to Darryl about Penny for a second, if you could—"

"Screw you, dickwad." The phone went dead.

JJ paced his room, the spring so tight he almost pulled out the last of the whiskey under his bed and chugged it. Before he could do that, he dialed again.

"Eff off, JJ. Mom doesn't want to talk to you, and I sure as hell don't." Patrick hung up again, and JJ went for the whiskey bottle.

WHEN MAGGIE woke him up the next morning for school, JJ felt like his head might pound itself open. He worried briefly that Maggie would take one whiff of his breath and go ape on him, but he'd been pretty careful with the toothpaste and mints last night. She didn't seem to notice. When she asked him if he was all right, he muttered something about his hand and she left the room to get ibuprofen.

He'd gotten really good at drinking alone in his room without Maggie noticing.

He pulled on dirty jeans and his "Shakespeare Hates Your Emo Poetry" T-shirt, which Maggie had gotten him for his last birthday. *Yeah, Shakespeare, you'll sure hate any poetry I come up with today*, he thought.

Math passed in murmurs and formulas JJ didn't understand. He had no idea how he was holding up a C- in that class.

He was looking forward to spending Creative Writing with Detective Finch and the Alabastor Restaurant Fire, but Ms. Lyle had a surprise assignment for them.

"Today we'll do some simple journaling—suspend whatever prose or poetry you've been working on. I'd like you to do some introspective writing. Consider this topic: write something no one else knows about you. As always, these are your private journals, so the only way anyone else will see this entry is if you choose to workshop it with the class."

Ms. Lyle pulled out her own journal, which she sometimes wrote in as she walked around the class observing them, and everyone else started scribbling.

JJ stared at the blank page. Something no one else knows? Wasn't there usually a reason for that?

"Everything all right, JJ?"

Ms. Lyle stopped above him, and JJ wondered if any teacher actually wanted a legit answer to that question. Probably not, he thought, so he decided to give her one.

"No."

Ms. Lyle didn't even react, though. She just tapped his pencil with hers. "Sounds like you have lots to write about, then."

Fine. She wants what no one else knows? I could give her a list.

THINGS NO ONE ELSE KNOWS
By Jacob Jasper Jones

1. I can't look at my scars for more than two minutes without wanting to throw up all over them.

2. My father may hate me up in heaven.

3. There's a good chance my mother does too.

4. I'm ruining my Aunt Maggie's life.

5. I barely know my sister, Penny. I barely know her because I'm never allowed to see her. (A couple of people know that.)

6. My sister Penny got adopted, but no one wanted me. (A couple of people know that, too.)

7. Darryl adopted Penny but she wouldn't take me because even then I was a troublemaker. (Let's just make this a list of things not too many people know.)

8. I beat up her son.

9. The reason why is actually something no one knows except Patrick and me. So I'm not gonna write it here. Until he tells, I never will. Never.

10. I was only six. I didn't think it would be such a big deal.

11. I was really mad. Even angrier than when I found out about Mom and Dad.

12. After that, Darryl stopped the adoption process on me. Not Penny. Just me. She said her kids couldn't live in fear of me.

13. Dennis, the older one, didn't have a problem with me. He knows Patrick is a douche bag. (Okay, everyone knows that.)

14. Since Darryl and Mom were best friends, she said she still wanted to take care of Penny, for Mom. But she said she couldn't trust me anymore.

15. I think she really always wanted a girl anyway. I was just another boy. She already had two!

16. Then Aunt Maggie had to come back from her big National Geographic assignment in Asia to take care of me. Grandma's mind was already going by then. The Alzheimer's was getting really bad. She couldn't even remember Mom and Dad were dead.

17. Aunt Maggie and I moved into Grandma's old house. They sold my house, the one I lived in with my parents. I'm really glad they did. I could never have lived there again. Ever.

18. Aunt Maggie was only twenty-two. She didn't know what to do with me. We ate a lot of pizza that year and she got a job doing wedding photography.

19. I think that was why Maggie didn't adopt Penny and me right after the fire—she was too young. She liked being a photographer for National Geographic.

20. Darryl still really wanted to be Penny's mom. Maggie let her. Probably because she couldn't handle having a baby. That still makes me really mad sometimes. I was supposed to be able to see Penny anytime I wanted to, but it hasn't worked out that way. Darryl still doesn't trust me with Penny.

21. Darryl still owns the used clothing store she and my mother used to own together. Sometimes I walk by it on my way home from school, even

though it's not really on the way. Sometimes I just want to go in there and yell at her, remind her that I had only been out of the hospital for a few months when the fight happened, and I still had nightmares. Part of me wants to tell her what Patrick said that got me so angry. But I won't. And it wouldn't help anyway. I heard her husband make a bunch of those excuses for me the night before Darryl kicked me out. She didn't care. She just kept saying they "couldn't take the risk" and "Marilyn would have understood."

22. Marilyn was my mom. I know she wouldn't have understood.

23. Jacob was my dad. He probably is rolling over in his grave (and Mom too).

24. I miss them. I miss my mom and dad, and most of the time I have to miss my sister too.

25. People wonder why I don't like to answer questions or talk very much. There just isn't much good to say.

JJ looked up from his notebook to find the classroom empty. Only Ms. Lyle was still there, grading papers at her desk.

"Ms. Lyle?"

She smiled. "Oh good! You're done. You were so intent you didn't even hear the bell ring. I always think writing that important must be too good to be stopped, and I had my planning period anyway...." She began scribbling something on a piece of paper. "What do you have next? I'm writing you a pass."

"Umm... Biology."

"Okay." She handed JJ a piece of paper as he was gathering up his books. "I truly look forward to the day when you share your writing with the class, JJ."

JJ didn't. Of course, he also didn't look forward to handing Mr. Butler (or Coach Butler, as all the football players referred to him) a flamingo-colored pass that said "Scribbling with the creative muse."

BY MONDAY, JJ's mind was on the court hearing for his trespassing charge, which was already scheduled to take place that Wednesday morning. JJ didn't ask how Maggie had magically made that happen so quickly after their conversation in the police station. Maggie knew a lot of people in their small town because of her photography business, and JJ didn't doubt that she had pulled some strings for him.

"Man, you ever gonna dress out for gym?" Tom Whitmore was standing next to him, lacing up his sneakers. "This will be, like, the third week in a row you haven't dressed out. You know you're gonna fail, right?"

"So?" JJ shrugged and pulled his journal out from the pile of books next to him on the gym bleachers. "I failed it last year too."

Tom laughed. "Dude, you're crazy."

Tom was one to talk. The last time he and Tom had partied together, Tom had ended up jumping off a roof into a lake just to prove that he could. That was a hell of a lot crazier than failing gym.

The gym teacher ran over to the bleachers. "Class is starting in a minute or so. You ever going to join us, Jones, or shall I just jot the F into my gradebook now?"

JJ scowled. Coach Dallows wasn't the same teacher who had failed him last year, but he might as well have been. JJ wasn't sure why he still bothered to show up to the class and sit on the bleachers; by this time last year he'd started skipping the period altogether and spending it in the bookstore down the street.

"Fine," JJ mumbled into his shoes.

"That's not really an answer. You know, I talked to the counselor about you. I understand your aunt tried to get you out of the course and everything. You know by now that isn't going to happen. You have no medical conditions to prevent you from taking this course, and every student who is physically able to do so takes PE at Watkins High. You won't graduate without this course, Jones, so you may as well start dressing out for it."

JJ stared at the wall until the teacher walked away to blow on his whistle a few times and call for stretches. Maggie had tried, she really had, to get the counselors to remove the PE requirement from his schedule. It hadn't worked. They just insisted JJ could wear sweatpants, and claimed JJ was wrong when he said that would make even more people ask questions, because no one wore sweatpants in PE. Like Coach Dallows had said, JJ was physically able to participate, and so he would take the course until he passed it.

He was never going to pass it, though. He would fail out of Watkins before he would put on shorts and show off his scar-covered calves to a gym class of thirty students.

"JJ, WHAT are you wearing?"

"What?" JJ scanned his outfit. Jeans, a Shins T-shirt. He liked it.

"We're going to court, JJ. While I'm sure it's not formal, you look like you're headed off to some kind of indie music festival. Try to remember that appearances do matter at these sorts of things, okay?"

Sometimes JJ forgot that Maggie actually knew what an indie music festival was. "I don't own anything else," he mumbled.

"Sure you do." She marched over to his closet and came back with a blue polo shirt and khakis. "Lest your legs actually become denim."

JJ stared at the shirt, wondering where it had come from.

"I bought it for you before school started," Maggie said, as if she could read his mind "Heaven knows why. C'mon, get changed. We're going to be late."

JJ's lawyer had arranged for them to meet directly with the judge—it was something called court diversion—and from what JJ understood, all it meant was he wouldn't have to have an actual trial. He should have been relieved, but he was actually pretty disappointed. He'd wanted to see if trials looked the way they did on TV. It might have saved him some research for future Morris Finch stories.

The conference room in the courthouse was cinder block, with a long metal table and uncomfortable metal chairs surrounding it. JJ sank into one. His lawyer and Maggie were speaking in whispers beside him. All JJ could make out was words like "service" and "no prior record."

He tried to keep his breathing even so his heart wouldn't pound quite so much.

A large, overweight man in a blue suit and red tie came in through the door, along with a uniformed black police officer JJ thought looked familiar. The man in the suit seated himself at the head of the table, placing a large briefcase down and popping it open with great authority. JJ realized he must be the judge.

"Good morning. I'm Judge Henry Elson; this is Donald Favor, the arresting officer. Do you remember him?" JJ thought the judge must be talking to him, and he nodded, even though his memory of the guy was sketchy at best.

The judge pulled a thin manila folder from his briefcase and flipped through it. "Let's get right to it. We're here and not in the courtroom because this boy has no prior record and was involved in no particularly malicious behavior on the night in question?"

"That's correct, Your Honor." JJ was surprised to hear his lawyer answer for him. "Mr. Jones admits he was trespassing on the property, but he meant no harm whatsoever. He was merely sitting on the roof when Officer Favor found him."

The judge looked at the officer, who nodded.

"Fine, fine. Jacob?"

Maggie nudged JJ hard in the side, and he realized the judge was talking to him again. "Sorry. Everyone calls me JJ. Yeah?" Then Maggie nudged him again. "Yes?" JJ corrected.

"Can you explain your activities of that evening, Jaco—JJ?"

JJ forced himself to make eye contact with the judge. Holding his hands in his lap so no one would see them shaking, he cleared his throat. "I just wanted… a place to be alone. The theater is kind of important to me. Someone told me you could use their fire—" His voice caught around the word fire. "—escape to get to the roof from the outside. I was just going to hang out there for a while and go home, but I guess someone saw me."

"Officer Favor?"

"He certainly didn't appear to be involved in anything else." Officer Favor's voice was deep, almost intimidating. "He was just sitting there. Didn't move much when I pulled out the cuffs, either."

JJ remembered being a little too buzzed to do anything else.

The judge glanced down at the file again. "Would you mind explaining why the theater is so important to you?"

JJ opened his mouth to speak—and no sound came out.

His lawyer spoke for him. "It's my understanding, Your Honor, that JJ's parents were both killed in the Bijou Street Movie Theater fire ten years ago."

The room grew quiet. JJ thought Officer Favor shot him a sympathetic look, but it was hard to tell under the man's hard expression.

"I see." The judge closed the file. "JJ, do you understand the seriousness of being arrested for trespassing?"

JJ cleared his throat. "I sure do now, sir," he said quietly. The judge and Officer Favor laughed, and Maggie squeezed his hand nervously.

The judge began writing something in a file. "Mr. Dawes." He looked at JJ's lawyer. "Would you and your client be amenable to six months' probation and fifty hours of community service? I hope for this young man to remember the seriousness of his crime and feel less inclined to repeat the error in judgment."

JJ's lawyer looked at Maggie, and she nodded eagerly. JJ sighed to himself. Fifty hours of community service. Oh well. He had a feeling from Maggie's slight smile that it could have been much worse.

On the drive home, Maggie squeezed JJ's shoulder protectively and babbled on about his community service sentence.

"This could actually be really good for you, Jaje. I'm always saying you should participate in more after-school activities, and maybe you'll end up working someplace you like. I was thinking about Parks and Recreation, or one of the elementary schools, or the court has a list of options...."

She went on, but JJ was really only interested in one thing. "Maggie, do you think Darryl will let me see Penny now? Since they let me off with community service?"

Maggie turned the car into their short driveway. "I'm having lunch with her tomorrow, JJ. I promise I'll do everything I can to convince her. Everything I can."

IT WASN'T enough.

JJ knew it the second he came through the door Tuesday afternoon. Maggie was sitting at the kitchen table drinking tea, the defeated expression on her face making her look a lot older than she was.

JJ sank into the chair next to her. "So no, huh?"

Maggie smiled sadly. "She's worried, JJ. She's convinced this arrest thing will continue to be a pattern."

That wasn't promising. "So, how long until Penny can come over again?"

"Until you finish your community service. Darryl says if you can do that, you'll prove to her you're taking your transgression seriously."

JJ jumped up from the table. "But fifty hours is going to take forever! Penny will forget who I am by the time I'm allowed to see her again!" JJ could feel the spring tensing and pulling within him. Didn't Darryl *understand?* Didn't she get that Penny felt like the only thing JJ had left of his old life, the life before the fire?

Maggie pulled him back into his seat. "Don't be so dramatic. Penny won't forget you. I do agree that it's far too long. I suggested we compromise at twenty or so hours. She wouldn't hear it. She said when you've finished all your hours, she'll know she can trust you with Penny."

JJ crossed his arms and concentrated on keeping his breathing even. "This is such bullshit! What does she think I'm going to do anyway? Lead Penny into a life of crime? Teach her to rob banks? We're not even alone when I see her!"

Maggie chortled. "Banks, eh? That's what I'd be worried about. I can just see my ten-year-old niece robbing banks…. 'JJ, grab the gun!'" She mimicked Penny's high, youthful voice, and JJ found himself laughing along with her for a moment.

"You'll just have to rush through that community service as quickly as possible," Maggie said as she took another sip of her tea. "Decide what you'd like to do. Tomorrow we'll make phone calls… oh shoot. That reminds me. I need to call the hospital and arrange to have your stitches removed soon."

"Wait…." JJ went over to the fridge and took down the card Dr. Ben had given him. "Dr. Ben said to call him to do it."

Maggie took the card and half smiled. "You must have made an impression, JJ." She picked up her cell phone and left the room, calling behind her, "It's nice to hear it was a good one."

JJ snorted and began hunting for an afternoon snack. He couldn't believe Darryl. He missed his sister and wanted to see her, and he knew Penny probably wanted to see him too.

So he'd just have to find a way around Darryl.

CHAPTER 4

OPPORTUNITY APPEARED the next morning, after another gym class that JJ had read through. JJ waited alongside the row of lockers on the second floor of the high school's A building: prime locker location. Only seniors got these babies, which were within perfect proximity of almost every class. JJ's locker was out in the C building, and he didn't even bother to use it half the time. It was an Everest-sized hike just to get from there to science class.

"JJ?" Dennis walked up next to him and began twisting the combination lock. "You looking for me?"

"Well, I sure don't have a locker here." JJ stepped back a little as someone moved in to use the locker he was standing in front of. "I was wondering if you could help me out with something."

"I can try." Dennis pulled some books from his locker and shut it with a quick slam. Dennis was blond and tall, like his father, but his long, lean face held the same sharp, angular features as his mother. "But I think I already know what you're going to ask me."

"You do?"

"Sure. You're going to ask me to get Mom to change her mind about you seeing Penny."

JJ stepped back again as the hall around them filled with students. "That'd be great, if you could… but actually, no. That's not what I was going to ask."

Dennis looked puzzled. Above the din of chatter around them, he asked, "What, then?"

JJ tried not to look sheepish. "Look, dude, I really wanna see Penny. And we both know Darr—your mom isn't going to change her mind anytime soon. I was wondering if maybe you could help me kind of see Penny on my own...."

But Dennis was already shaking his head. "No way. My mom would find out, and she'd ring both of our necks. It's not worth it, JJ."

JJ felt like ringing Dennis's neck. "Not worth it?" He nearly shouted. "Dennis, do you have any idea what this is like for me? Your mom's gonna keep punishing me the rest of my life for something I did when I was still a little kid, and Penny, too! Penny already lost her parents, now Darryl's gonna take me away from her too?"

"Look," Dennis said calmly. "I'm not saying it's not a raw deal— for both you and Penny. And I get what you're saying about the risk." His brow knitted in thought, and JJ felt some hope rise within him.

"I know...," Dennis muttered to himself. Then he said aloud, "Look, JJ, here's what I'm going to tell you: be at the public library at 4:10 this afternoon."

JJ was wary. "Why? Even if Penny's there, won't Darryl be too?"

Dennis sighed. "You're gonna make me spell this one out? Fine. Penny's having a little trouble with reading. Ma got her a tutor—one of the juniors here who's part of that elementary outreach program—and they're supposed to meet at the library at four today. I know for a fact Ma has to go get Patrick from karate then, so she won't be with Penny at the library most of the time."

JJ actually considered hugging Dennis. Four? He could do that. He didn't have his doctor's appointment to get his stitches out until tomorrow, and the library was in between his house and the school. It was perfect.

"Dude, thank you so much. I owe you big time."

The warning bell rang, and Dennis turned to leave. "No sweat... just forget I ever told you, okay?"

"Already forgotten," JJ muttered as he sprinted off to his next class.

THE LIBRARY was a quiet, comfortable place. It was close enough to the house that Maggie had often walked him there for reading programs when he was young, and JJ still went there once a week or so. The best inspiration for his Detective Finch stories was a good Colton Parker or Hamish Macbeth novel. He even liked Sherlock Holmes.

He had a hunch Penny would be in the Children's Room, which was basically the whole second floor of the library. He turned the corner at the top of the staircase and immediately saw her sitting at one of the study tables in a corner.

She could have been a miniature version of their mother, with her reddish brown wavy hair and bright blue eyes. It was a combination JJ rarely, if ever, saw. Penny even had their mother's slight build, and she was also short for her age, just like their mother, who hadn't made it over five feet two. JJ had his father's dark eyes and hair so dark brown it was almost black. JJ's father had been a sort of medium height and build, and it was looking like JJ was going to repeat those features as well. Everyone had always said JJ was a carbon copy of their father and Penny was a carbon copy of their mother.

Penny was bent slightly over the table, reading aloud. The person she was reading to was engrossed in whatever Penny was saying, leaning over the book to stop Penny every few seconds. It took JJ a minute to realize he knew the guy from Creative Writing class. It was McKinley Smith.

JJ didn't know—or want to know—the names of a lot of kids he went to school with, but he definitely knew McKinley. McKinley was a kid who *everybody* sort of knew. He was easygoing and smart, always talking in class and likely to strike up a conversation with you in the hallway for no reason. He was either in (or the president of) about a zillion clubs, and he had started the school's first Gay-Straight Alliance. Which made sense, because he was gay.

It was sort of a mystery to JJ how, in a backwoods corner of Vermont, McKinley Smith had managed to make being gay in high school *cool*. He always had a cluster of girls surrounding him, plenty of guy friends from a bunch of the different school cliques, and absolutely no problem being exactly who he was.

He fit in way better than JJ did, that was for sure.

Every day he sat in the front row of Creative Writing wearing Converses, jeans, and some random band T-shirt. Very often it was a T-shirt that JJ also owned, and JJ had thought a few times that they must have pretty similar tastes in music. His shaggy blond hair was always hanging in his face, and he liked to make complex comments about writers like Molière. JJ found it hard not to admire someone as self-assured as McKinley. And the guy was only a junior— just a year older than JJ.

JJ waited until McKinley and Penny had finished the page they were working on before he walked over, trying to work up a confidence he didn't really have. "Hey there, Penny."

"JJ!" Penny stood up quickly and threw herself into his arms for a hug. "I haven't seen you in forever."

"I know," JJ murmured into her hair. She was getting taller, but she still didn't reach past JJ's chest. "I think you've grown a little."

Penny pulled away and shrugged. "I'm still like the shortest girl in the fifth grade." She rolled her eyes. "What are you doing here?"

"Oh... you know, checking out books. I saw you and thought I'd say hello." He tried to keep his voice steady as he spoke; he wasn't a very good liar.

"Cool. This is McKinley, my tutor."

"Yeah... don't I know you from somewhere?" McKinley frowned slightly at JJ.

"Creative Writing class."

"Right!" McKinley snapped his fingers in sudden understanding and pointed at him. "You're the kid who never talks."

"Um. Yeah." JJ felt himself blushing.

"How do you know Penny?" McKinley looked puzzled.

"He's my brother!" Penny announced proudly. "We just don't live together. He lives with Aunt Maggie."

"Oh." McKinley studied JJ, but he didn't pry. "Well, JJ, Penny and I are just working on some of her homework together. You wanna stay and hang out with us?"

"Sure," JJ mumbled, shrugging as if that wasn't the best sentence someone had said to him in weeks. "I'd love to."

Penny worked on reading some passages from her social studies book and answering questions about them. McKinley had Penny read each passage aloud, stopping her whenever she tripped over a word or missed a line. Sometimes he also stopped Penny to ask her a question about the line she'd just read. JJ quickly realized Penny's reading problem was a little deeper than he'd thought when Dennis had first mentioned it that afternoon. How long had this been going on?

JJ almost didn't notice when it hit 4:45, signaling that Darryl could return at any moment. "Uh, I have to go," he said.

"Already?" Penny reached out for a hug, and JJ returned it, just as something occurred to him. Penny couldn't tell Darryl about JJ showing up at the library.

"Penny? Could you do me a favor?" JJ knelt beside her and spoke softly, hoping McKinley wouldn't catch everything he was saying. "Could you not mention to your mom that I ran into you today?"

Penny scoffed, making her look older than her ten years. "Of course not, JJ," she said with exaggerated emphasis. "She'd be so upset with me for talking to you."

A knife stabbed slightly into JJ's chest when Penny said that, but he tried to shake it off. After all, he'd seen her. He'd spent time with her. That was all that mattered, right?

JJ turned to leave, but McKinley called out to him.

"Bye, JJ," he said. "We have a lot to talk about tomorrow in school." His mouth was turned upward in a half smile. Had he heard what JJ said to Penny?

Whatever. Who cared if he had? JJ had already considered coming clean with McKinley and asking if he could show up at Penny's tutoring sessions more often.

He took off down the stairs before Darryl could appear.

JJ EXPECTED McKinley to approach him at the end of class the next day, but McKinley just waved at him as he left the room with someone from the girls' soccer team.

Huh. When was this conversation of theirs going to take place?

It ended up being lunchtime. JJ and Lewis were sitting with the group of skateboarders they usually ate with, and Lewis was telling JJ about another party that weekend. "This one's going to be epic. The weather's supposed to be decent, and Shelley's got a great house—"

Lewis was interrupted by McKinley, who slid into the chair next to JJ. "Hey, JJ," he said brightly.

Lewis blinked. No one as popular as McKinley ever came near their lunch table.

"Hi?" It came out as a question. JJ cleared his throat and tried again. "Hi, McKinley."

"I thought we should talk." McKinley popped the top on a can of soda and pulled a sandwich from a lunch bag. "Lewis, you mind giving us a few minutes?

JJ was pretty sure the only reason Lewis nodded and started talking to the other guys was because he was still shell-shocked that someone as popular as McKinley Smith knew his name.

"You didn't just happen to be at the library last night, did you?"

JJ scowled. "What are you talking about?"

"What you asked Penny at the end. Up until then I had you pegged as the perfect brother. Then you basically say that you're not allowed to see your sister, which means you were crashing our tutoring session. Which means I could get in a lot of trouble and lose my job over you showing up like that. I don't know if you know this, dude, but Darryl's a little crazy."

Of course JJ knew that, but it had never occurred to him that McKinley could lose his job. Not that it would have mattered if he had thought of it. JJ would have fired McKinley himself if it meant he got to see Penny.

"What do you want me to explain?" JJ murmured, more into his cheeseburger than anywhere else.

"Why aren't you allowed to see Penny? And are you trying to get me fired?"

"I'm not trying to get you fired." JJ felt like that might be the most important point to make. "Definitely not. I just wanted to see my sister again. Her adoptive mom and I don't get along so well, and she sort of cut us off from seeing each other for a while. I came to the library just to check up on Penny, say hi."

McKinley took a bite of his sandwich. "Why'd she cut you off from Penny?"

"Darryl thinks I'm a bad influence. That I get in trouble too much."

"Do you?"

JJ shrugged. "Yeah," he murmured. "But nothing really bad," he added more clearly. "And I really do want to see my sister. She's kind of like all I have left besides my aunt." McKinley didn't reply to that, so JJ assumed he already knew their parents were dead. "I think I should have a right to see my own sister."

McKinley sighed. "Look, JJ, here's the problem. I like your sister a lot, and so far you seem like an okay guy. But I really like tutoring, and I need the money for college. You can't keep showing up like that. Once was no big deal, but it can't happen again."

"No." JJ knew he sounded like he was begging, and he didn't even care. "I need to see her. I promise I won't get you in trouble. Penny wants to see me too, so she's not going to say anything. I'll be really careful and I'll make sure Darryl doesn't find out. Please? Not for the whole hour or anything. I just want to keep coming by to say hi, to listen to her read… that's it."

McKinley frowned at JJ; JJ started some silent begging again. *Please… please… please….*

"Okay. I'll tell you what: we'll make a deal."

"Okay."

"You can show up, as long as you don't get in the way of our session and you don't get caught by Darryl. If you do, I'm playing dumb. I had no idea you weren't supposed to see Penny; you're on your own. Got it?"

JJ nodded hopefully. So far, this didn't sound like a bad deal at all.

"But you have to do something for me."

"Okaaaaay…." JJ dragged the word out as long as he could.

"You have to agree to workshop something in Creative Writing."

JJ snorted. "Uh, no way."

McKinley shrugged. "That's my deal, JJ. Everyone in class is dying to know what you're doing in class all secretively over there. You share your stuff, I let you see Penny. It's that simple."

He left, and JJ sat there, wondering how much his solitude was really worth.

"Ew."

Dr. Ben pulled the last of the thick black thread from JJ's palm and began rubbing the area with some kind of liquid. "I know it looks strange," said Dr. Ben, concentrating as he placed a bandage on JJ's hand and secured it with tape. "Sort of like having these hairs pulled directly out of your body."

JJ smirked, and Maggie grimaced.

"All set." Dr. Ben smiled. "Keep the bandage on for a few more days, but overall the injury seems to have healed nicely."

"Thank you, Dr. Ben." Maggie began gathering her purse and coat. "For the medical help, as well as for contacting the police."

Dr. Ben smiled wryly. "They told me they were going to get in touch with you. What's been going on with that?"

JJ told him about the sketch artist. "But then the detective called a few days ago and said they'd sent the sketch to all the tattoo parlors in the area, and nobody had a record of doing that tattoo. Detective Starrow said that could just be 'cause it was so long ago, or it could be that guy actually had it done at home or did it himself, though. She said they looked into a lot of artists' communities when the fire happened, what with the turpentine thing, but now they're going to look back into those leads again and see if anything comes up." JJ shrugged and tried not to look as gloomy as felt about that conversation. "Basically, telling them didn't do shit."

"JJ!" Maggie said, but Dr. Ben laughed.

"Maybe not yet, JJ. But it's like you said: it's something new. We don't know yet what it could lead to."

"Yeah." That line of thinking was the only thing that had kept JJ from stealing one of Maggie's bottles of wine out of the kitchen cabinet after Detective Starrow had called.

"And it certainly was nice of the detective to let you know what they'd found so far."

JJ nodded. That *had* been nice. And she'd promised to call him again if anything new came up. It was good to know that adults didn't suck 100 percent of the time.

Which gave JJ an idea. There was another adult standing in front of him who also didn't suck, and JJ needed to get started on his community service soon. It would be really nice to do that with people he didn't want to kill most of the time. "Dr. Ben?" JJ couldn't believe what he was about to ask. "You don't need anyone to do community service for you, do you?"

"Excuse me?"

Dr. Ben and Maggie were both staring at JJ. "Well, I have these community service hours I have to do because I was on top of the movie theater, and I guess that's trespassing, and I thought maybe I could do some of them here." JJ stopped when he realized they were both *still* staring at him.

Dr. Ben cleared his throat. "I spend a lot of time in the Pediatric Ward, obviously. They are always looking for volunteers... people to spend time with the kids, cheer them up. It's not an easy job, JJ—you see a lot of sadness—but it's certainly rewarding."

Buried deeply somewhere in JJ's memory was an image of such a volunteer, leaning over him, trying to get him to talk, to eat. JJ stiffened.

Dr. Ben patted his shoulder. "Think about it. If you're interested, I'll get you set up with the volunteer coordinators."

On the way home, volunteering was all Maggie could talk about.

"Of course, I love the idea of you working for the hospital, but are you sure it's a good idea, JJ? You have so many memories of your own from that exact hospital." She winced a little, and JJ knew she was remembering his five-year-old face, dulled with pain and sadness, staring sightlessly at the walls of that same pediatrics ward. "I'm just surprised you'd want to work there."

JJ didn't answer. When he'd first asked about whether or not Dr. Ben needed help from volunteers, he hadn't thought about the fact that he might have to go back to Pediatrics again. But Dr. Ben was cool, and maybe working at the hospital would be good—help him get over those memories from right after the fire. Or something like that.

Or maybe not. Just thinking about the pediatrics ward made JJ wish he had another bottle of whiskey in his room. As soon as they were home, he texted Lewis and made plans to go with him to the party on Saturday.

CHAPTER 5

OCTOBER WAS a suspect time to have a keg party in a field in Vermont; you never knew what the weather might do. Lately it had been unseasonably warm though—Maggie kept calling it "Indian summer"—so JJ just grabbed his windbreaker on the way out of the house Saturday night.

"Have fun!" Maggie called after him. She thought he was going to Lewis's house to play cards with some of the other guys. JJ was glad she'd ended his grounding a few days ago and he didn't have to try and sneak out of the house.

JJ and Lewis met at their usual corner and walked to Rick Mooring's house. Rick was one of the guys from their lunch table who was old enough to drive. After seven people had managed to pile into Rick's mom's minivan, they drove off to a cow pasture on the edge of the next town over.

Music was already blaring from someone's car stereo when they pulled up beside a line of other vehicles. JJ jumped out and was pleased to see two kegs stacked side by side next to an old building. He was on his way there before Lewis could even make it out of the car after him.

The second the first sip of beer was down his throat, he felt that tightly wound spring relax within him and start to unwind a little. He would have rather had whiskey, but beer would definitely do the trick.

For a while JJ was content to hang out by the kegs with Lewis, Rick, and their other friend Todd, downing cup after cup of the cheap beer. He saw Rick swig down a few and knew he should wonder who was driving them home, but he didn't.

JJ was coming out of the bathroom in the house when he saw McKinley. He was sitting on a sofa, drinking out of a blue party cup like JJ's, surrounded by his usual harem of women. Only JJ wasn't sure if you could consider it a harem if the dude wasn't sleeping with any of them.

Maybe it was the beer, but JJ found himself staring in that direction a little too long—and eventually McKinley saw him. He got up from his spot on the couch and came over. "Fancy meeting you here."

JJ gestured to the loud, crowded scene around them. "'Sa party, isn't it?"

McKinley nodded. "C'mon," he said finally. "Let's go for a walk."

JJ staggered after McKinley down a pasture to a small cow pond. McKinley sat down on a large rock and pulled JJ down after him.

"You're pretty drunk. You know that, right?"

"Am... I?" JJ was pretty sure he was. Walking had been pretty tricky, and now he was having trouble focusing on McKinley's face.

McKinley shook his head. "I hope you know how you're getting home."

JJ looked around for Lewis. "My ride... somewhere...."

"You didn't workshop your writing yesterday."

JJ was startled out of his stationary search for Lewis. "Not yet. I'm not... ready yet. Monday, maybe."

"What's the big deal?" McKinley asked. "What are you hiding over there in the corner every day?"

JJ tried to explain it through the fog in his head. "'Slike... they're my thoughts. Just mine. Don't want to share them with people. Don't want people to know... my stuff."

"I guess I don't get it. I mean, I write some really private shit I would never share with our class, but there are lots of pieces I write that I'm fine with the class reading."

JJ considered that. "Everything I write is me, so it all matters."

McKinley looked startled. "Wow. I never thought about it that way. You're just that private, huh?"

"I guess...." JJ tried to focus his vision on a tree in his line of sight. Things were starting to move a little too quickly around his head, and he was getting dizzier. He thought for a second about the dream, which he'd had again the night before. "I mean, I share some things. Like I told Dr. Ben about the tattoo guy. That was private."

"Tattoo guy? Huh?"

"The guy... from the fire. With the tattoo. I told Dr. Ben... I remembered him. That was private. Only I knew I saw him."

"JJ, are you talking about the fire that killed your parents?"

"How'd you know?" JJ could hear the accusation in his voice, only he wasn't sure what he was accusing McKinley of.

"Everyone remembers the fire, dude. Penny's mom told me that your parents died in it, when I started working with Penny. Course, she never told me about you."

"Oh." JJ was calm again.

"So? Is the fire where you saw the tattoo guy?"

"Yup." JJ popped the end of the "p" between his lips. "But no... no one knows where he is. He's invisible." JJ couldn't help but laugh uncontrollably. "The guy who set the fire was invisible!" Soon he was hysterical, laughing like a hyena into the murky, dark water in front of the rock.

"I think it's time to get you home." McKinley pulled at his arm.

JJ instantly pulled away. "Look, I'm not gay, okay? Get your hands off."

McKinley rolled his eyes. "Listen, kid, as tough as it is not to be totally attracted to your drunk and disoriented ass, I promise that I'm not coming on to you here, okay? Just trying to help you walk."

JJ frowned. "Okay, but nothing else, okay? Just walking."

McKinley shook his head, and JJ thought he murmured something about every guy in the world thinking they were the hottest thing around whenever a gay dude showed up.

Then Lewis was there too, dragging the other side of JJ. He heard Lewis swear. "I think Rick left without us."

"We'll have to walk!" Somehow this was hilarious to JJ too, and he heaved with laughter as he tried to amble away from Lewis.

Hands held him still. "What are we going to do?" Lewis sounded like he was pleading.

"I could take you home," JJ heard McKinley say. "Just as long as JJ keeps his stomach together in my car. It's my mom's."

"I'll watch him," Lewis promised.

JJ closed his eyes, and a few moments later, he opened them to find Lewis next to him in the backseat of a strange car. "Lewis?" he muttered.

"'Sup, dude."

"I think I'm... drunker than I usually am."

Lewis had been drunk with JJ a lot, and he didn't hesitate a second. "You sure are, dude."

"What 'bout... Maggie?"

Lewis frowned. "I think I may have to sneak you in again."

JJ heard McKinley's bemused voice from the front seat. "I think I'm starting to see what Darryl sees in you, JJ. You really are trouble, aren't you?"

JJ wanted to argue with that, but suddenly he couldn't get his tongue to move.

McKinley dropped them off at the corner and wished Lewis luck getting JJ into the house. They edged around the bushes at the back of house, Lewis holding JJ's mouth to keep him from laughing, until they reached JJ's bedroom window. It was on the first floor, and JJ never locked it, just in case he needed a good route back into the house. Lewis shoved the window frame up and, after quickly checking for watching neighbors, he was able to hoist a limp, laughing JJ up over his shoulders and shove him through the window frame.

JJ landed with a loud thump on his bedroom floor. Something hurt, but he didn't know exactly what.

"JJ?" Lewis was calling from outside the window. "You in okay?"

"Yup." JJ dragged himself up to look at Lewis out the window. Lewis was tugging on his wrist and muttering something to himself. He looked annoyed.

"McKinley said I was trouble," JJ told Lewis over the windowsill.

Lewis laughed, already concentrating on something on his cell phone screen. "Well, yeah, dude, you are. That's why I hang out with you."

JJ only had a few moments to ponder this before he passed out on the floor under his windowsill.

JJ WOKE up Sunday with nausea, a splitting headache, and the pattern of the wood floorboards ground into his right cheek. Most of the previous night was a blur. He remembered talking to McKinley, but what had he said? He remembered something about telling McKinley he wasn't gay, and then not much afterward. The one thing he remembered clearly was McKinley's comment in the car that he was "trouble."

What surprised him was how much those words kept stinging as they rolled back and forth through his head. Why did he care so much what McKinley thought?

JJ blinked. Wait—did that make him gay? Did he like McKinley or something?

JJ shook that thought off right away. People cared what other people thought of them all the time, right? You didn't have to be into someone to care what they thought about you.

Except JJ almost *never* cared what anyone thought about him. So why was McKinley's comment bothering him so much?

The truth was that JJ had wondered before if it was weird that he wasn't all that into girls. But he'd tried not to think about it too much. When Lewis and his other friends started making comments about boobs and stuff like that, JJ kind of just played along and pretended that the *Playboy* magazines they stole from their dads were really fascinating. Still, he told himself, *that* didn't mean anything. After all, it wasn't like he got totally turned on looking at guys, either.

Maggie had told him a few months ago, when JJ had said there weren't any girls he wanted to ask out, that he was probably a late bloomer. Well, maybe he still was. And JJ just cared what McKinley thought because McKinley was his key to seeing Penny. Yeah, that had to be it.

Pulling himself up off the floor and onto the bed, JJ held out hope Maggie hadn't heard his loud entrance last night. There was nothing like a lecture to really turn up the notch on a hangover.

He stayed in bed until almost noon, leaving only for an occasional glass of water from the bathroom tap. Maggie came in around ten to make sure he was still alive, affirming that she hadn't heard JJ's awkward arrival the night before. JJ told her he was just tired, that he'd stayed out too late last night, and he wanted to sleep. She accepted that and went back to her work.

Eventually JJ pulled himself out of bed and grabbed his Creative Writing journal from his backpack. Despite the blurriness of last night, he also remembered telling McKinley he would hold down his part of their deal.

JJ flipped through the book, looking for something, anything, he could share with the class.

Morris Finch. No way. People who knew about his connection with the Bijou fire would be all over him.

His "Things No One Else Knows" list? No way.

An entry about Penny? Definitely too personal.

There was something written about how much he liked whiskey. Didn't really seem appropriate.

Everything was just so... him. He'd have to write something else. It would still be a part of him, but it needed to be a part of him he could at least say out loud.

He grabbed a pen from his backpack and thought. About the dream, about psychologists who said JJ was "defiant" and "depressed," and about teachers who gave him detention when he wouldn't answer their questions... and about what McKinley had said last night. Finally, he wrote.

Broken

Sticks and stones, they told me
Break bones, they told me
Words, they told me
Don't hurt, they told me

The words have come
Always, with fire behind them
The fire of bad news,
And anger,
And problems

I have responded to these words
With a fire of my own
Fire that brings more words
Of bad news,
Of anger,
Of problems

I know no other response
Their words
Have broken me

It was him. But disguised enough, shrouded enough, that he thought he could actually read it.

JJ didn't usually read or write a lot of poetry, but now he thought he understood why people liked it so much. It was the perfect opportunity to say exactly what you wanted in a way that only you could understand.

Code. That's what poetry was. A sort of genius code for writers.

THE POEM was a success.

Mrs. Lyle clapped her hands when JJ raised his hand to share his writing with the class, and then she clapped again when he was finished reading. McKinley just grinned at him from across the room, causing JJ to squirm in his chair.

There were a few critical comments—suggestions of word changes or possible syntax revisions—but most of the things people said were positive.

There was one comment, from a serious boy named Andrew who sat in the corner of the room, that stayed with JJ.

"I wonder....," said Andrew, tapping his pencil against his lips as he spoke. "The poem is really about a cycle, isn't it? Words that bring fire, fire that brings further words? Much as I love the title, I almost feel the greater theme of the poem is that unbreakable cycle. Shouldn't that be included in the title somehow?"

The class had murmured in agreement, and JJ had left the room thinking.

Andrew had noticed something in the poem, something JJ had never been able to see in his own life: that he might be trapped in a cycle. And it was more than just the cycle of teachers hating him when he didn't talk to them, even though JJ thought that was an important part of the bigger problem. No, this cycle was *everything.* Everything JJ did. Everything McKinley was referring to when he'd called JJ "trouble" the other night. From the moment JJ had heard the worst words he'd ever hear—"Your parents didn't make it"—to his fight with Patrick, to his silence in the school shrink's office, to stealing the dead frogs after someone had called JJ's attitude "disturbing"... the cycle just kept going.

His whole life was an unbreakable cycle.

He spent the first half of biology class wondering if maybe it wasn't unbreakable. If maybe he didn't have to be so angry all the time, and always getting in trouble, and constantly making Maggie crazy. If maybe he didn't need to be the reason his parents were rolling over in their graves.

But how did you break a cycle when the cycle was *your whole life?*

So while his teacher droned on and on about mitochondria, JJ took out his poem and examined it again. He thought about one line he'd written: "The fire of bad news."

Could you end a cycle by going back to where it started? JJ was supposed to start volunteering in the Pediatrics Wing of the hospital that weekend. He'd be going back to where he'd first heard the horrible news about his parents.

Maybe he'd figure out something there. Maybe going back to the beginning of the "fire of bad news" was what he needed to do to be... JJ wasn't sure what the word was. Happy? Not pissed off every moment of the day?

Whatever the word was, the idea felt so encouraging that JJ actually opened his book and started taking notes.

CHAPTER 6

"WELCOME TO the pediatrics ward."

The Volunteer Director scanned the crowd of five people standing before her. JJ ducked, worried she would see his shaking hands and decide there was no way he could handle this assignment. Ever since he'd workshopped his poem earlier in the week, he'd been looking forward to this. Looking forward to seeing if this volunteer work was what he needed to do to somehow break the cycle. But the moment JJ had reached the familiar front entrance of the Pediatrics wing, a flood of memories had poured through him, and the spring had wound painfully in response. It was all he could do not to turn around and run the other way. The cheerful walls seemed to be laughing at him. He fidgeted, accidentally nudging into a middle-aged woman next to him. She glared at JJ before focusing back on the director.

"As a volunteer for this department, your job is essentially to be a companion to the children here." The director swept out her arm to indicate the row of open doorways behind her. "Many of these children are lonely. Many are in pain. Many do not have family that can visit constantly or consistently with them, so they need strong companionship...." She began to walk them down the hallway, going on about what they could do for the children in the ward, but JJ wasn't following what she said.

He had gone far enough to see into the first door on his left. There were four children in it—all boys. Three of them were happily sitting up in bed. One appeared to be reading, and the other two were watching TV.

The fourth boy wasn't doing anything, though. He was lying down on his stomach, staring at the wall. His face was ghostly pale and JJ could see from the way his hands were drawn into fists that he must be in pain.

Suddenly JJ was sure that he was going to vomit all over the spotlessly clean linoleum in front of him. He turned from the volunteer group and ran.

"Son?" The director was calling for him, but JJ barely heard her. This had been a really stupid idea.

He'd barely pushed his way out of the swinging doors of the ward when rough hands caught his shoulder. "Hey!"

JJ glanced up long enough to see Dr. Ben towering over him, looking puzzled. "What's up? Shouldn't you be touring with the group right now? I just came to see how your first day was going."

JJ's stomach was churning. "I'm going to be sick."

Dr. Ben tugged him down the hall, and JJ went willingly. He allowed Dr. Ben to gently push him through a door and into a stall in the men's room, where JJ lost all of his lunch and breakfast almost instantly.

Eventually JJ heard a knock on the stall door, reminding him that he wasn't alone. He pushed open the stall door, feeling shaky and embarrassed. "Sorry," he muttered.

"Nothing to be sorry about. Are you okay now?"

JJ leaned against the metal next to him, trying to catch his breath. He hadn't even made it past one door in the ward. "Fine," JJ said quietly. "I just… saw something, that's all." Dr. Ben would probably think he got sick at the sight of blood.

But Dr. Ben looked concerned. "What was it?"

JJ stared at the floor, stubbing his toe into the white tile.

"Let's go down to the cafeteria. Get you some ginger ale." Dr. Ben tugged again on JJ's sleeve. For some reason, JJ followed.

In the cafeteria, Dr. Ben ate tomato soup. JJ drank ginger ale and nibbled on crackers. His stomach already felt better, but Dr. Ben had suggested he take it easy on food for the moment.

"You gonna tell me what caused that visceral reaction you had back there?" Dr. Ben slurped some soup.

JJ fidgeted, eyes on everything in the room but Dr. Ben. "It was a stupid idea," he muttered.

"Well, that answers everything." Dr. Ben smiled wryly.

JJ sighed. "I don't know why I thought I could volunteer there." What the hell had he been thinking?

"I was surprised you wanted to work here, JJ. I'm guessing you spent a lot of time in the pediatric ward, didn't you?"

JJ's voice was so hoarse it didn't even sound like his. "I was in one of those beds for weeks—I don't even remember how long."

Dr. Ben studied JJ's dark expression. "Then why on earth *did* you agree to volunteer there?"

"Well, at first it was just 'cause I don't like most adults very much, and you're pretty cool, but then I wrote this poem and I realized that I'm, like, in this stupid cycle or something, and I started to think that maybe once I was here I could figure out how to break it or something. Since this is where it probably started." JJ took a long breath and shook his head. "See? Stupid."

"What cycle? What are you talking about?" Dr. Ben was clearly confused.

JJ rolled his eyes. "The cycle! The stupid cycle of me being angry all the time. Of me being trouble!"

Dr. Ben's mouth turned upward in a grin. "What are you smiling about?" JJ snarled.

Dr. Ben picked up his napkin. "Nothing. It's just… teenagers. You think you're the only people in the world."

JJ hadn't been expecting that answer at all. "What?"

"You think you're the only one who's angry? You think I wasn't angry when Sara died? When I brought my beautiful daughter for a fun day at the movies, and never came home with her? When my relationship of years and years ended because it couldn't survive losing a child? You think I'm not angry too, JJ?" Dr. Ben's voice was quiet and smooth, never wavering.

JJ felt like Dr. Ben's cool demeanor had squashed his temper tantrum. "Maybe, but you're not pissing people off all the time."

Dr. Ben shrugged. "Maybe not. But I also wasn't five when that fire happened. Look, JJ, don't get me wrong—anger can tear you apart. I'm quite certain it destroyed my relationship. But it's about how you react to your anger, what you choose to do with it. I've spent my life trying to put that energy into saving other people. I hope that if I do that well enough, it will make up for the anger I have that I couldn't save my daughter. I applaud your effort to look for ways to improve your life and your own choices, but to start in the Pediatrics Ward? If I had the scars you do, both physical and not, that would be a lot for me. I know that much."

Feeling numbed by such a speech, JJ could only mumble. "Well, what am I supposed to do now? I still need my community service hours. And most adults really don't like me all that much."

Dr. Ben laughed. "Look, there are lots of other departments in this hospital that need volunteers, JJ. And I just happen to know the folks who run the Physical Therapy department well. I also know they're in desperate need of volunteers. Why don't you let me talk to them for you? I'll warn them you're a little… intense."

"*Intense?*"

"Hey, doctors are used to intense people. We're pretty intense ourselves. Plus, in that department, you'll probably just be wiping down tables or something. And don't be so hard on yourself. I really am glad you're thinking about the choices you make, but you don't need to fix everything that's wrong overnight. Get some more crackers down and I'll take you home."

JJ shrugged and took another cracker, studying Dr. Ben's words in his mind.

THAT MONDAY, at the library, JJ wondered if his sneaking around to see Penny counted as part of the cycle. He decided it didn't. He wasn't sneaking around to see Penny to get back at Darryl or something—he just wanted to be part of his sister's life. What could really be so wrong about that?

At exactly 4:10, JJ was at Penny's table in the Children's Room. "JJ!" Penny squealed, and JJ thought he saw McKinley smile slightly at him.

JJ watched McKinley walk Penny through some reading aloud, which seemed a little less terrible this week (or maybe JJ just wanted that to be true). McKinley even let JJ read the last section of one of Penny's chapter books to her.

At exactly 4:45, JJ got up to leave. Penny was bent over her backpack, looking for something in her folders.

"Hey," McKinley whispered to JJ. "Hang around. I want to talk to you after Penny leaves."

JJ thought about ignoring him, but he didn't really want to piss off the only connection he currently had to his sister. So instead he loitered in the Mystery section, looking over a few Agatha Christie novels. He'd never thought they looked all that interesting before, but Aunt Maggie insisted she was one of the best writers of all time. He was bringing two of her books up to the counter when he had to duck back behind a display of DVDs: Darryl had arrived.

Darryl probably looked like any other middle-aged woman to the other patrons of the library, but from JJ's perspective, she might have been a vampire racing into the library to suck the blood of everyone there.

Of course, even Maggie admitted that Darryl had an intimidating presence. She was average height, but she had nearly perfect posture and tended to wear high heels, so she always looked tall. She had the same sharp, angular features as her son Dennis, and she dressed in lots of dark colors. On top of all that, her hair was such a bright shade of red that JJ sometimes wondered if she dyed it.

When JJ was eight, he had told Maggie that Darryl could go out on Halloween without a costume and everyone would just think she was a wicked witch.

JJ stayed hidden behind his DVD stack until Darryl came down the steps from the Children's Room with Penny behind her.

"Did you and McKinley get a lot done today?" she was asking Penny sweetly. JJ was always astonished at how just how drastically Darryl's tone could change. When she spoke to JJ, she always sounded angry and annoyed, like he was a telemarketer calling to interrupt her dinner (he'd only tried that trick a few times).

"Good! We're two days ahead in work, and we did some reading in my chapter book for extra...." Penny's voice drifted away as she and Darryl left through the library doors, and JJ breathed a sigh of relief before stepping out from behind the shelf.

JJ checked out his books and waited for McKinley on a bench just inside the front entrance of the building. He was already into the second chapter of one novel when McKinley abruptly sat beside him. "Whatcha reading?"

JJ studied McKinley briefly, trying to decide whether to tell him. "Agatha Christie."

"Mystery. Hmm. So your reading tastes match your persona?"

JJ squinted. "You think I'm a mystery?"

"Well... you barely talk in class, and it turns out you're actually this really great hidden poet. Not to mention you're the secret brother of the kid I'm tutoring. Sounds pretty mysterious to me."

JJ grinned at the idea of being mysterious. "Speaking of mysteries... whatcha want to talk to me about?" He narrowed his eyes. "You remember that I'm not gay, right?"

McKinley sighed. "Sheesh, JJ. Do you tell every girl that you ever meet that you're not interested during the first five minutes you're talking to her?"

JJ frowned. "I don't really...." He stopped himself from admitting that no girls had ever really interested him. "Ah, no."

"Good. Then take my advice, and don't do it with every gay guy you meet either. Listen, the reason I wanted to talk to you is that the other night, at the field, you were babbling a little." JJ blushed, not quite sure exactly what he'd been babbling. "You were talking about how you remembered the guy who might have set the fire. You kept calling him the tattoo guy."

Of course. He would have said that. "Yeah... so what?"

"So you don't start babbling shit like that to some person that you barely know without getting them interested. I wanna know more. What did you mean when you said no one knows where the tattoo guy is?"

JJ frowned. "Listen, McKinley, I was drunk, okay? I don't even remember what I was saying. So can we just drop it?" He grabbed his backpack and stood.

McKinley crossed his arms. "No."

"Excuse me?"

"No. Listen, JJ, everyone in Moreville remembers that fire. It's a really big deal. And then you start talking about how you might know the guy who did it or something? You can't just decide not to tell me the rest of that. I mean, you're not the only one who loves a good mystery."

JJ snorted. *You'd like them a lot less if you lived through mine*, he thought. "Whatever."

But McKinley kept his arms crossed and his eyes on JJ. "JJ, I'm already taking a really big chance on you, letting you show up to my sessions with Penny like this. So if you want to keep this arrangement going, you gotta trust me too." His mouth stretched into a half smile.

JJ blinked. "Are you... blackmailing me?

McKinley waved that off. "Only a little. And JJ, I'm really not doing it to be an asshole or something. I do want to get to know you better. I think you're an interesting guy." He patted the seat next to him.

JJ shook his head and sat back down. "I'll tell you a little," he finally compromised. "But I'm still not gay, okay?"

McKinley studied him with that same half smile. "JJ, methinks you are starting to protest too much."

JJ just rolled his eyes.

He ended up filling McKinley in on the same basic details of the dream. McKinley nodded as JJ talked, looking more interested when he got to the specific details of what the tattoo looked like.

"They even did a sketch of it?"

"Yeah. They sent it out to the tattoo shops and whatever. So far, nothing."

McKinley nodded. "Dude, that sucks. So what are you gonna do now?"

"About what?" JJ was puzzled.

"To find the arsonist. You know, solve the mystery." McKinley gestured at the novel on JJ's lap.

"You think *I* should look for the guy?"

McKinley shrugged. "I dunno. Just kind of seems like you're all about mysteries and stuff. Plus, even if the police are looking into the tattoo, there's no way it can be their first priority. That fire happened a decade ago. I thought someone who created an arson investigator as the key character in his writing would be all about finding an arsonist he's dreaming about. "

"How do you know about Detective Finch?" JJ was appalled.

McKinley shrugged. "You have your mysteries, I have mine."

"That's… private! I told you, I'm really private!" JJ sputtered.

"Yes. Yes, you are." McKinley nodded earnestly.

JJ was speechless.

"Seriously," McKinley continued, "you seem all about this detective stuff. So why not give it a go? I'm not suggesting you charge into dangerous back alleys or something. But this is a small town. There's gotta be something about that tattoo we could look into."

"*We?*"

McKinley shrugged. "JJ, I'm not gonna lie. I'm a little bored these days. It's not like there's a lot of dating prospects for a guy like me in this Podunk town, and I'm sick of spending every weekend either drinking in a field or going to the town's one bowling alley. Even Twitter's boring right now. Our school's classes are way too easy." He smiled. "I asked you about the stuff you were spewing in the field that night because it seemed like it might be interesting. And it turns out I was right."

JJ found that he was still speechless.

"Look, think about it, okay? I know you'll be at Penny's next tutoring session. We can talk about it then." And with that, he punched JJ lightly in the shoulder and left.

JJ was pretty sure his mouth was wide open. And he still couldn't come up with a single thing to say—not that there was anyone there to say it to, anyway.

PENNY'S NEXT tutoring session wasn't for two more days. JJ spent those days trying not to make eye contact with McKinley in Creative Writing and doing a whole lot of his trademark thinking.

He was sitting in writing class the day of Penny's session, trying to make revisions to his poem. He'd already decided that Andrew was right about the title, and now "Unbreakable Cycle" was scrawled across the top where "Broken" used to be.

Their words have broken me.

He studied the line for a long moment. He still hadn't decided if he believed this cycle was unbreakable. Dr. Ben had said something in the hospital about how he was glad JJ was thinking about his "choices," and JJ thought he should probably try to do more of that, but that couldn't be all it would take, right? Just thinking about the choices he was making seemed way too easy. The cycle JJ was talking about in the poem felt so much bigger than that.

JJ started to change the line in the poem around, playing around with the idea of *settling a score*, the phrase he'd heard Maggie use in the hospital.

I know no other response but to settle the score

And then, all at once, it was there: the answer.

If he *was* stuck in a cycle, then *of course* going to the hospital hadn't broken it—that wasn't where the cycle had really started. The cycle had started with the fire, with the moment the arsonist had walked into the Bijou Theater.

Maybe that was the only way to break the cycle: settle the score with the arsonist.

Instantly, JJ decided that McKinley was right. JJ should start looking into the tattoo himself. Honestly, he wasn't really sure why he hadn't thought of that before. With all the hours he spent reading and writing mystery stories and watching cop dramas on TV, it should have occurred to him to do some of his own investigating. And McKinley was also probably right when he said the police weren't going to put their full attention on catching someone who started a fire years ago and had never been heard from since. No, if JJ really wanted this cycle broken, he was going to have to start looking for this tattoo himself.

JJ played with a few more words in the poem and sat back to consider whether he wanted McKinley's help. And when McKinley glanced over and waved, JJ decided it was time for a pro-con list.

CONS:
—Have to talk to McKinley a lot and tell him personal stuff
—I like doing stuff by myself
—I don't think he believes that I'm not gay

PROS:
—Might be nice to have someone else know what's going on
—Could help me make some other friends
—He's really happy all the time

And for some crazy reason, it was the last item that convinced JJ he should take McKinley's help.

"SO WHAT do we do first?"

JJ just blinked. It was right after Penny's tutoring session that evening, and he and McKinley were sitting in a secluded section of the library, away from the Children's section, just in case Darryl and Penny came back to the library for some reason. JJ had just told McKinley he was up for them doing some detective work together… only to find out that if McKinley was bringing anything to the table, it sure wasn't years of knowledge and experience with arson investigation.

"How should I know?" JJ tried not to growl, but he was pretty sure he didn't end up sounding very nice.

McKinley just shrugged, undaunted by JJ's tone. "I mean, you read all the detective stuff. You even write it. I figured you'd know where we should start. What do the characters in books do first?"

JJ was still pretty annoyed that McKinley had found out about Finch, but he decided to let it go for the moment. Instead, he thought about what Detective Finch always did first. Detective Finch was based on hours and hours of crime dramas and movies and pages and pages of mystery novels, so that had to be at least close to right. "Um. They look over all their clues. They go back over the scene of the crime."

"We can do that." McKinley pulled out a notebook. "You talk. I'll write."

An hour and a half later, they'd run over everything JJ remembered from that night, everything he remembered from his dream, and a lot of the newspapers and police reports in the library's archives. McKinley sighed and ran his hands through his hair. "Wow. I'm starting to see why the police got stuck." He gestured at the notes and printouts around them. "That's not a lot to go on."

"Yeah," sighed JJ.

"So what do we do now?"

JJ thought back to one particular Finch story he'd written, where Finch hadn't had anything to go on from the crime scene. "We have to figure out what kind of person the suspect might be."

McKinley nodded. "Makes sense. What do we think?"

"Well, I've always thought that someone who tries to kill an entire theater of people like he did must have been kind of a grandstander. I mean, we know he was targeting Theater Three, so most people think he was trying to kill just one person, but does he just go after that person? Nope. He burns down a whole building."

"That's true," McKinley said slowly. "What kind of sick man does something like that?"

"Well...." JJ snapped his fingers. "The kind of person who can't resist going back to the crime scene!"

McKinley looked baffled. "What are you talking about?"

JJ couldn't tone down his excitement. "Sometimes when someone kills a bunch of people like that, they do it because they need attention. They need to feel important or something. So they like to go back to the scene of the crime—sometimes they even get involved in the investigation. They can't resist anything that reminds them of what they did, of how many people they hurt."

McKinley looked dubious. "Are you sure that's real, JJ? That sounds like something you saw on some cop show. "

JJ blushed because, yes, that was a pretty typical plot point on almost any cop show that involved a serial killer, and yes, JJ had seen a lot of those. "Yeah, I know, but I research a lot of stuff I see on those shows for my Finch stories. I did some research on whether or not people really go back to the crime scene for this one story I wrote a while ago. And they do. It's real."

"Wow." McKinley snorted. "That is… sick."

"Yup, it is." JJ frowned. "But I'm sure the police were watching the people who were involved in the investigation pretty carefully, so if he was one of 'em, they didn't figure it out. And people go to that movie theater, like, every single day. So I don't think that's going to help us."

"Unless we make going to the Bijou all about *him*." McKinley leaned across the table excitedly.

"Huh?"

"I mean, just going to the theater probably doesn't make him feel all that important—it's a rebuilt theater with a plaque in front of it. We need to make the theater a place that's all about the *fire,* and then he's almost guaranteed to come back to it."

"How do we do that?" JJ asked, and he realized he was leaning across the table now too.

McKinley tapped the table. "I can't even believe how perfect this could be! So, here's what I'm thinking. My mom's job is actually kind of to throw fundraising events. She works for a party planning company, so she throws a lot of them for people. Well, what if I asked her if anyone has ever done some kind of benefit for the victims of the Bijou Street Movie Theater fire—you know, since it was such a big deal in this town and all. I bet no one has in a really long time. I could suggest that one of the organizations she works with might want to do one, since we're coming up on the ten-year anniversary of the fire. We could make it a memorial. The guy would probably come to that, wouldn't he?"

So maybe JJ wasn't 100 percent sure that he wasn't gay. Because at that moment, he was definitely thinking McKinley was the most amazing, wonderful person he'd ever seen in his life.

It was the perfect idea.

"CHECK IT out."

McKinley said it with great gusto and handed JJ a folded piece of paper from his back pocket. JJ unfolded it.

Cordelia Events
Presents

A Night of Remembrance

A Memorial and Fundraising Event in
Honor of Those Who Lost Their Lives
Ten Years Ago in
the Bijou Street Movie Theater Fire

Join Us at the Bijou Street Movie Theater
For a Night of Music, Food, Memories, and a Silent Auction
All Proceeds Benefit Families of Victims of the Fire

Saturday, November 12th, 6:00 p.m.

JJ leaned against the locker he was standing next to. "Wow. Your mom put that together so quickly?" It was less than a week since McKinley'd come up with this idea.

"Sure. She's really good at her job." McKinley shrugged. "My dad says he thinks that being around all those invitations and table settings is what turned me gay."

JJ's mouth dropped. "Your dad doesn't like that you're gay?"

McKinley rummaged through his locker for something. "He's okay with it. I mean, I think he wishes I wasn't, but he still loves me and all. He's my dad."

"Wow."

McKinley studied him. "Why 'wow'?"

"I dunno." JJ shrugged. "It just seems like you have everything, you know? You're always happy, and everyone at school likes you, and your parents are good with you being gay. It's like you have the perfect life."

McKinley laughed and started walking to class and JJ followed. "JJ, I so don't have a perfect life. No one does." He paused for a second and put his arm around JJ, who immediately glanced around to make sure no one was watching them and getting ideas—but no one seemed to be paying any attention. "I just don't try to hide anything or be something I'm not. And I've been lucky—so far it's been going okay."

JJ decided to change the subject rather than talk about *that* too much longer. "Whatever. What if this fundraiser thing doesn't work out? What if the guy doesn't show up? Or we can't figure out who he is?"

"Then we all get some free food, and money gets added to your college fund."

JJ shook his head emphatically. "No way. Any money that anyone sets aside for my family goes right to Penny."

"Fine. In the meantime, what do you think? Of the invitation? My mom's all set to make it a go, but I told her I thought I should run it by a friend who could probably tell me what the victims of the fire would think."

JJ didn't love being called a victim, but that was something to consider. Would the other survivors of the fire want this benefit to happen? There had been a lot of fundraising events right after the fire, but now nobody was even talking about the fact that the ten-year anniversary was happening in a few months. JJ had noticed this was pretty typical when Something Horrible happened to a large group of people. For a while, everyone else was Desperate to Help, until enough time passed that they had to go back to their own lives. And then the people who'd been part of the Something Horrible were left on their own to put the pieces of their lives back together. JJ figured maybe life had to be that way, or the whole world would never stop being miserable. But it sure sucked for people who went through that original horrible thing.

"A lot moved away," JJ finally said quietly. "But maybe it would be good for some people. And some of the families could use the money—I know they could." He remembered one news article from a few years ago about a woman who was living in an old, beat-up apartment complex and trying to raise three kids by herself; her husband hadn't had life insurance.

"That fire ruined our lives," she'd told the reporters. "We lost everything when we lost my husband."

JJ could help make sure some of the money got to her.

"Yeah," he finally said decisively. "It's a good idea. I just hope it helps us catch the guy too."

McKinley looked smug as he tucked the invitation back into his pocket. "My mom should be able to get a lot of people there. The more, the better. For Penny's college fund."

He headed to class, and JJ spent the next few hours trying to figure out whether part of his unbreakable cycle was that he was trying to be somebody he really wasn't.

But how could you be someone you weren't without knowing it? Wasn't it impossible *not* to be the person you really were? Eventually the whole thing hurt JJ's head too much to think about, and he ended up actually paying attention in history class rather than trying to figure it out anymore.

CHAPTER 7

THE WEEKS leading up to the memorial were a whirlwind. JJ couldn't remember when time had passed so quickly.

He was working as many hours as he could in the hospital's physical therapy center, which had turned out to be a decent place. Dr. Ben must have told them what to expect from JJ, because no one there ever got upset when he answered them by shrugging or something. Anyway, it wasn't like the work was hard or required a whole lot of talking. Like Dr. Ben had predicted, he mostly just wiped down tables and helped patients from area to area. But it wasn't totally boring work, and he felt like he was accomplishing something—something good, even. He wasn't anywhere close to finishing his fifty hours, but he was pretty sure he was farther along than Darryl would expect him to be.

Every Tuesday and Thursday, he showed up at Penny and McKinley's table at exactly 4:10. Penny had told JJ that she and Darryl had been fighting a lot when Darryl tried to help her with homework, and Darryl thought it would be a good idea for her to have another "role model" to do her work with. JJ couldn't even feel bitter about being overlooked for that role. Darryl had never considered him a role model.

The sessions were fun, though. McKinley usually let JJ do Penny's extra credit reading with her, and JJ loved reading aloud to her. It was something he had missed out on when he was younger; he'd been banished from Darryl's house during prime reading-aloud-to-Penny years.

Every now and then McKinley would sit with him at lunch to give him new details about the benefit: who was coming, what the food would be. They formed a lot of different game plans for what they would do if they actually saw Tattoo Man, as they'd started calling him.

On weekends he and Lewis hung out. They partied a little, but JJ made a point to avoid places where McKinley might be. For some reason, JJ didn't want McKinley to see him sloshed again.

JJ might have started to think about the choices he made in his life and whether or not they were the right ones, but he wasn't giving too much thought to whether he should stop drinking. The spring was still there, always coiled, and sometimes it felt like a drink was the only thing that kept it slack enough for JJ to get through a day.

JJ was forced to remember how tight the spring really was a week before the benefit. Because that was the day Darryl caught him.

IT WAS a fairly ordinary day, all things considered: another silent session of Creative Writing with McKinley smiling at him once in a while from across the room (and what was up with all the smiling anyway? Was that just a gay thing?), another hour of PE spent on the bleachers reading Agatha Christie, who was turning out to be pretty good. The rest of his classes were uneventful. Normal.

He got to the library at 4:10. Normal.

He sat down at the table and watched Penny and McKinley work through a chapter in Penny's science book. He was in the middle of helping with one problem that Penny still wasn't quite getting when a hand clamped down on his shoulder.

The three of them all looked up from the book together, and JJ was sure their faces all held the same identical expressions of shock.

"Jacob Jones." Darryl's voice was so icy with contempt that JJ almost shivered. "What are you doing here?"

JJ tried to remain calm and ignore the spring. He'd need serious composure to lie here. "Um. Yeah. I was… here, you know. Returning a book. I saw Penny, so I came over. And then she and McKinley were working out this problem, so I thought I'd help…."

It was clear from Darryl's expression that she didn't believe a word he was saying.

"McKinley? Is this true?" Darryl kept her hand clamped to JJ's shoulder, but she managed to nail McKinley with a hard, fast look at the same time.

"He ran into us here...." JJ noticed McKinley was very careful with his words. "I didn't think it was a big deal if he helped, and Penny said he's her brother, so I said he could hang." JJ couldn't help but be impressed by McKinley's incredible poise and calm in the face of a raging Darryl.

Darryl turned her death gaze to Penny. "Young lady? You know there are times and places you are allowed to see JJ. You didn't inform either McKinley or JJ of this?"

JJ knew his little sister well enough to know how much she hated being in trouble. As Penny's eyes went wide and teary, JJ decided it was time to act like the big brother he wasn't usually around to be.

"Is that fair, Darryl?" JJ asked, standing up to meet her gaze. "What's she supposed to say? 'Mom won't let me see my brother, so I can't even say hi'? And how's her tutor supposed to respond to that, anyway? It doesn't exactly sound normal."

Darryl's eyes narrowed. "That is exactly what she is to say, JJ, and she knows it." Darryl's voice was soft and dark. "I know what's best for her right now. I'm her mother."

The spring was coiling more and more tightly within JJ. "I'm her brother, and I've never been anything but great to her. All I want to do is spend time with her, and you can't even let her have that. You're too much of a control freak." JJ tried desperately to keep the tone of his voice cool and even like Darryl's, and not let the anger overtaking him seep through.

Darryl laughed—a hollow, distant laugh. "Control freak?" She shook her head slowly, almost sadly. "If only she could remember what you did to my Patrick, she'd thank me a hundred times over for my caution."

JJ flushed at the memory of the one time he had truly lost his temper and let the spring snap—something he had never done since.

He needed to get out of that library before it snapped again. "Well, I was six years old, Darryl." *And you sure don't know what Patrick did to me first.*

"Bye, Penny." He squeezed her in a hug before she could hug him and get herself in more trouble. "Bye, McKinley. See you in school."

He left thinking about how much fun it would be to push Darryl off of her heels and down the stairs of the library.

Outside, a light, cold rain had started to fall, reminding JJ that winter wasn't going to avoid Vermont for too much longer. The temperature seemed to have dropped ten degrees since JJ had gotten to the library less than an hour ago. Too bad he only had his windbreaker with him.

JJ started up the deserted sidewalk in front of the library, taking deep breaths and trying to calm down. Damn, he needed some liquor. None of Lewis's usual crap, either. Jack Daniels. What had he just *done?* Finally lost it on Darryl, that's what he'd just done. Which meant he'd lost any chance to ever see Penny again, probably. He'd definitely lost these afternoon tutoring sessions.

Which meant he'd probably lost McKinley too.

JJ remembered McKinley's clear promise that he wasn't having JJ ruining his job tutoring. And now, just like JJ ruined everything else, he'd managed to ruin that too.

That thought just made JJ's stomach clench more tightly. Would McKinley even speak to him after this? Was this the end of lunches, and the smiles across the classroom, and talking about the benefit? JJ scrubbed his face and started charging up the sidewalk, not even sure where he was going. Of *course* McKinley wouldn't speak to him after this. He'd said from the start that JJ was trouble. JJ just kept proving it.

It was about that time that JJ realized he had tears running down his face.

He rubbed at them and kept walking, almost unaware of the soaked clothing that was making him shiver. Why was he so upset about that? It wasn't like McKinley was his only friend. In fact, he barely knew him. But he just couldn't escape the fact that the idea of not seeing McKinley anymore—of not talking to him—was winding JJ's spring more and more tightly.

It was winding it as much as the idea of not seeing Penny was. And JJ had never remembered wanting to spend time with anyone as much as he wanted to spend time with his sister.

Oh God. Maybe he really was gay. This wasn't like the time when Lewis stopped speaking to him for three days because JJ had made fun of him in front of some other friends of theirs. JJ had felt horrible then, and the idea of losing Lewis as a friend had upset him. But it wasn't like this. It hadn't wound JJ's spring like this.

JJ fidgeted anxiously as he walked. He needed somewhere to go. Strangely enough, he actually wanted someone to talk to. There was Lewis's. Lewis would have some liquor, which would help with the spring. But Lewis and JJ never talked about anything *real*. No way was JJ telling Lewis that McKinley might have turned him gay.

There was always Maggie. Maybe she'd even lighten up and let him have some of the wine she kept on hand. But JJ wasn't really interested in talking to Maggie about how you knew if you were into someone. Anyway, Maggie was meeting with her group of other wedding photographers tonight. It was a semi-annual meeting they held to discuss changes in the market and technology, and it usually lasted well into the night. If JJ went home now, it would be to an empty house.

The problem was that the person JJ really wanted to talk to probably wasn't speaking to him. And might never speak to him again.

That really only left one person who might understand anything that JJ was thinking about or feeling—maybe not about the whole gay thing, but at least about some other important things.

JJ ducked into a drug store where he used his cell phone to find the address of Dr. Ben Peragena. Dr. Ben's house was probably about two miles up the big hill that headed away from Moreville. JJ pulled his chilly, wet arms inside the front of his shirt to keep a little bit warmer, and started walking. Hopefully he'd find a liquor store. And someone over the age of twenty-one who felt like buying alcohol for a teenager.

He didn't. He also didn't find a better jacket waiting magically for him on any of the street benches he passed, and as the rain and cold steadily ground themselves into his body, and as the sky grew darker and darker, he sure wished one would appear.

By the time he was a few blocks from Dr. Ben's address, he was already questioning the decision-making skills that had allowed him to walk over two miles in rain and near-freezing weather. His teeth were chattering so quickly they seemed to be getting numb—just like the rest of his body. His feet kept shuffling along below him; otherwise he wouldn't have even known they were there.

Just as he was considering turning back (and wondering if that was an even dumber idea, since it would be an even longer walk back), he discovered he was on Dr. Ben's block.

JJ rang the doorbell and tried to pull his front teeth back together.

The door opened, but it wasn't Dr. Ben standing before him. Instead, it was a tall, older, athletic guy, with short blond hair and piercing blue eyes. He was dressed in exercise clothes. "Can I help you?" he asked mildly.

"Uh... I was looking for Dr. Ben?" JJ was trying desperately to hold his shivering body together. He hadn't considered that Dr. Ben might not live alone.

"He's not here right now. He's still at the hospital, I think. Is there something I can do for you?"

JJ's spring had never felt so tightly wound. He wasn't allowed to even talk to his own sister; Aunt Maggie was gone; his friends were useless; he couldn't talk to the one guy he really wanted to talk with, who might also be the reason he'd turned gay. And now even Dr. Ben, who JJ also barely knew, wasn't there. JJ had felt completely alone many times in life, but never more so than when he'd been lying in that hospital bed and Aunt Maggie had told him his parents hadn't survived the fire. Later on, thinking about those weeks, he'd thought that he would never feel that kind of loneliness again.

But he'd been wrong. Here it was again, on a totally normal evening, ten years later. Almost as though his parents were dying all over again.

JJ turned from the door before this total stranger could see tears appearing in his eyes, but the guy called out for him. "Wait! He should be home soon. Why don't you come in and wait, warm up? You look like you're freezing."

JJ stopped. More cold rain splashed across his shoulders, and he decided he really wanted to be *warm* again.

He followed the blond guy into the house, which was larger than JJ had expected. It had a large open living room filled with comfortable-looking furniture and a very expensive-looking stereo. There was a tall staircase stretching above the room, and JJ could see it led to an extensive second floor.

"Warm up for a bit, okay? What's your name?"

"JJ," he murmured, wondering again what he was doing there. He'd made another stupid mistake.

"I'm Jeremy. I'll call Ben and tell him you're here." Jeremy headed toward a bright room off of the living room, where JJ could hear him talking quietly. "Yes—no—no, he just showed up. It looks like he walked; he's soaked. No, I didn't ask. I'll check. Yeah, I'm on it. You'll be home when? I'll tell him."

Jeremy came back to the living room. "He wants to know if your aunt knows you're here." JJ shook his head. "Oh. Then he wants you to call her."

JJ shook his head again. "She's gone tonight. She won't be back until later."

"Oh." Jeremy was studying him carefully, as though JJ were a map he was trying to figure out. "He wants me to tell you to take a shower to warm you up while you're waiting for him. He said I could grab some dry clothes for you, and he'll be home in about half an hour anyway."

JJ was about to object when another set of chills ran though his shivering body. A warm shower *would* feel good. "Thanks," he murmured.

Jeremy led JJ up the stairs to a bright white bathroom with an enormous tub, and found some dry sweatpants and a sweatshirt for him. "How do you know Dr. Ben?" JJ finally asked.

"Oh. I'm Ben's ex." Jeremy headed back down the stairs.

Dr. Ben was gay?

JJ just stood there for a minute, staring at the door Jeremy had closed behind him.

JJ wasn't the type to believe in fate. If fate existed, that meant his parents were always going to die, so... well, he didn't like to think about that.

But this? It seemed almost too *fated,* or something, to be real. On the exact same evening that JJ realized he might have feelings for a guy, he'd gone to Dr. Ben to talk (something JJ never wanted to do before), and he just happened to find out that night that Dr. Ben was gay? And this was in a town where, like, five people (or that's the way it seemed to JJ anyway) were anything other than straight?

It was *crazy.* Just crazy enough to make JJ wonder if maybe it wasn't fate—maybe it was a sign. Did the universe really send signs? JJ thought things like that only happened in movies.

JJ remembered Dr. Ben saying he broke up with someone after the fire. Was this the guy? Had Dr. Ben been gay for that long? If you were gay, were you gay for your whole life? But that couldn't be right, because JJ was pretty sure he hadn't been gay before he met McKinley. So maybe Dr. Ben also hadn't always been gay? Or maybe JJ always had been and just never knew it? JJ really wished he knew the answer to *that* question. Well, maybe now he could find out—it looked like Dr. Ben *could* help out with some of JJ's questions.

JJ stayed under the shower for a long time, letting it warm him all the way through to his bones, before he finally decided it was probably time to get out.

The clothes Jeremy had given him were too big, so JJ rolled up the cuffs and sleeves. After his long walk in the cold rain, they felt like the softest, most comfortable things he'd ever worn.

He spent a few moments trying to decide what to do with his soaked jeans and shirt, and he finally hung them up in the shower. Hopefully they would dry a little before he went home.

Halfway down the stairs, he could see Dr. Ben saying good-bye to Jeremy at the door. Jeremy closed it behind him, and Dr. Ben turned, smiling when he saw JJ.

"Oh good! Walking pneumonia hasn't set in yet."

Walking pneumonia? Did that actually exist?

Dr. Ben gestured for JJ to have a seat on the couch where he was sitting, but JJ stayed standing. "You're gay," he blurted out.

Dr. Ben nodded. "Yes, I am. Is that going to be a problem?"

JJ shoved his toes into the carpet. "No," he finally mumbled.

"Good." Dr. Ben gestured to the seat on the couch next to him. "So what brings you to my neck of the woods soaking wet?"

Memories of the argument with Darryl flooded back through JJ, and he found himself gritting his teeth against them. "Dr. Ben, you don't happen to have a beer I could have a few sips of? It warms me up." He tried to look as pathetic as possible.

"Beer warms you up?" Dr. Ben looked amused. "No, I don't have any. However, I do have some hot tea ready for you. Let's see if that can do the trick." He went into the kitchen and returned with a steaming mug. "It's raspberry soother. My mother always made it for me."

JJ tried it. It could use some more sugar, but overall it wasn't too bad. It did warm him up right away, but it definitely didn't have the effect a nice sip of whiskey would have.

"So? You gonna spill, then? What are you doing here, JJ? What happened tonight? What was so bad that you took the trouble to find my house?"

JJ shrugged and took another sip of tea.

Dr. Ben sat, waiting.

JJ couldn't figure out why he didn't want to say anything. Hadn't he come here because he wanted somebody to talk to? He thought about all the teachers and shrinks over the years who had practically begged him to talk. Tonight, he'd finally wanted to. So why wasn't he?

It took him a few minutes, but eventually he did. He talked.

About beating up Patrick when he was six and about Darryl never ever forgiving him.

About never getting to see Penny. About Darryl saying he couldn't see her again until he completed his community service hours.

About sneaking into the library. About McKinley being Penny's tutor.

About his confrontation in the library. About storming out and walking all the way to Dr. Ben's house.

When he finished, the raspberry soother was almost gone, and the only thing he hadn't mentioned were his thoughts about McKinley.

Dr. Ben grinned as JJ compared Penny's expression while he and Darryl were fighting to the look someone has while they're watching an intense tennis match. "You know, you are certainly right in that respect, JJ: this Darryl person has definitely made things difficult for Penny. Penny obviously wants you in her life."

"I think she does." JJ finished off his tea. "But how can she, really? She doesn't know me at all. She's seen me like once a month for a few hours almost her whole life. I'm like that divorced parent that only shows up for birthdays and holidays."

"Maybe so. Darryl really thinks you're a threat somehow?"

"That's what she said again tonight." JJ mumbled into the empty mug. "That was okay. Do you have any more?"

Stretching, Dr. Ben walked to the kitchen. "You know, it's interesting—if you hadn't told me about that incident with Patrick, I would have thought she was trying to keep you away from Penny out of jealousy."

Intrigued, JJ followed Dr. Ben into the kitchen. "She's jealous? Of me?"

"Sort of. Well, maybe." Dr. Ben filled a kettle with water and set it to boil on the stove. "It sounds like she always wanted a daughter, yes? And then, this beautiful girl falls in her lap—just happens to be the daughter of her best friend, so she gets to do something good there too. Only here's the son, who remembers his parents well, and probably won't want his sister raised with a brand-new mother."

Understanding stretched its way through JJ's mind. "You mean… it was easier for her to be Penny's mom if I wasn't around to always remind Penny Darryl wasn't her mom?"

"Maybe. I'm just saying that could have something to do with it. Although I'm sure you beating the crap out of her son didn't help the situation."

JJ shrugged. "I didn't beat him up that bad. I mean, I still think she blew the whole thing up way too much. Anyway, it doesn't matter now. That's definitely the last time I'll see Penny for a while."

"Are you sure?"

"Definitely." JJ slammed the mug down on the kitchen counter so suddenly that the dish towel on the edge seemed to jump. "I can't do anything right," he murmured.

"What do you mean by that? Seems a little harsh to me." JJ was surprised to see how unruffled Dr. Ben remained. *Don't worry, you'll screw up eventually and scare him*, he reminded himself.

"*You* know." JJ made it an accusation. "I heard my aunt telling you that day you stitched my hand up… my dad's turning over in his grave because of me. I'm pissed off, and I just mess stuff up all the time."

Dr. Ben nodded. "I see. So you think you screwed up big today, huh?"

"Course I did. She caught me."

"It never occurred to you that maybe you did the right thing this afternoon?"

"Huh?" JJ didn't think he'd ever heard those words in his life.

"Well, think about it. The other day in the cafeteria you were telling me you've figured out you might be stuck in a cycle, yada yada yada. Today, this woman, Darryl. She gets you all mad. In the past, you've beaten up her son when you got upset. Today, though, you're calm. You're cool. You're respectful. You say your piece and you leave before you can get too angry." He raised his tea mug as if he were saluting JJ. "An excellent reaction. Sounds like a cycle breaker to me. I bet your parents would be proud."

"But she's still mad. I mean, I didn't apologize or anything."

Dr. Ben nodded as he poured more tea for JJ. "You think it would have been the right thing to apologize? Is that what your parents would have wanted?"

JJ thought about that for a moment. About the stories Maggie told of how his father had once stood up to a huge guy in a bar when he wouldn't leave Maggie alone. About how his mother was known for being this incredibly nice person who also made sure people listened to her. He knew that when a bank had refused to give her and Darryl the loan for their store, his mother had somehow talked them into it.

"Huh," JJ finally said.

"See? Look, JJ, I haven't known you very long, but I have already managed to learn two things about you. One, you do have some anger going on there. I get that. Two, you have decided that, on some level, you want to do something about that anger. I *very* much appreciate that. However, you have to remember that the world isn't black-and-white all the time. Sometimes there aren't good guys and bad guys—just guys, doing the best they can."

JJ took a long sip of raspberry soother and thought about that.

"It's like I told you the other day—nobody fixes all of their problems overnight. You should give yourself some points for identifying a problem, period. Those are the first steps in programs like Alcoholics Anonymous, you know."

JJ flushed a little, wondering if Dr. Ben was remembering his earlier request for a beer.

"What say we go watch some mindless TV for an hour or so? It might clear your head, and *Scrubs* is on Netflix now."

"You watch *Scrubs?*"

"Sure. That show cracks me up. They've got a lot of hospital life right, too...."

THEY WERE a few episodes in before JJ finally got up the courage to ask the other question that had been on his mind all evening. "Dr. Ben... how did you know you were gay?"

Dr. Ben looked at him curiously, but didn't press why JJ was asking—just pushed pause on the remote. "Well... I wondered first. I always wanted to be with guys more than girls. I wasn't very interested in girls, and the first time I tried to kiss one, I didn't really enjoy it. I knew I was gay when I met the first guy I wanted to kiss, I think. And I definitely knew for sure after I kissed him." He studied JJ for a moment. "Any particular reason you ask?"

JJ couldn't seem to stare anywhere but at his mug. "Well, I didn't tell you everything about tonight. McKinley? The guy tutoring Penny? He's gay. Like, really gay—out at school and everything. And we've been spending a lot of time together. Tonight, after the fight, I realized he probably won't want to talk to me anymore, since I ruined his job and all. That made me really upset. I'm just... starting to wonder... you know? Maggie just said I was a late bloomer or whatever, because I'm really not interested in going out with a girl or whatever." He dropped his gaze to the floor. "But McKinley. I think maybe he's turning me gay or something. Because tonight, when everything went to shit, I really wanted to talk to him… and other stuff."

"Ah." Dr. Ben nodded in understanding. "So you came here instead."

JJ nodded.

"JJ, I know this is easier to say than to do, but I think you need to worry about labels a little less. Gay, straight, bisexual—they're just words. Who you like is who you like. Who you want to spend time with is who you want to spend time with. And people don't turn each other anything. If you like McKinley, it's because you're wired to like McKinley, not because he made you something you're not. My advice would be to let yourself do what you want to do, and see what you learn along the way."

JJ scoffed. "Dr. Ben, whenever I let myself do what I want to do, it doesn't go good. I mean, look at what happened today."

Dr. Ben rolled his eyes. "JJ, we've talked about this. I really think today was actually a positive step for you. And this guy, if he knows and cares about you at all, will likely see it the same way."

"Maybe. I don't know. I mean, he has done a lot for me. It was his idea to hold this memorial…."

Dr. Ben sat up sharply. "Wait. The memorial at the theater that's coming up? You have something to do with that?"

"Yeah, McKinley kind of set it up."

Dr. Ben raised his eyebrows. "No kidding? Did he hear Penny's story and want to do something?"

"Sort of." JJ kept his eyes on the arm of his chair. "I mean, I talked to him a little bit."

Dr. Ben eyed him suspiciously. "JJ, is there a reason you're having such a difficult time making eye contact during this conversation? What's going on during that benefit? I hadn't decided yet if I was going to attend or not, but your current behavior is really making me want to come with a bulletproof vest. What's up?"

That made JJ snort. "Nah, nothing like that. It's just that we sort of have a plan for that night. We came up with a plan to find the guy."

"Guy?"

"You know, Tattoo Man. The guy from my dream. The one I think is the arsonist."

Dr. Ben's eyes went wide. "What?"

"McKinley—I sort of told him about Tattoo Man. We think this guy might just be crazy enough to show up to a sort of reunion like that. Return to the scene of the crime and whatnot... then we catch him."

Dr. Ben's voice sounded strangled when he finally spoke. "Are you nuts?"

"Huh?" JJ sat up quickly in his chair. He'd sort of thought when he decided to tell Dr. Ben everything that Dr. Ben would appreciate the plan.

"I said, are you nuts? You have planned a whole event hoping you can catch a murderer?" At least he didn't sound angry. Just... really incredulous.

"Kind of. I mean, we're not really planning it; McKinley's mother is."

"McKinley's mother captures murder suspects for a living? Is she also a policewoman?" Now Dr. Ben looked a little angry.

"Huh?"

"Because if she's not, you're putting everyone attending this event in grave danger! What are you going to do if this guy does show up: pull out your handcuffs? You're fifteen, JJ! You are talking about potentially capturing the person who murdered your parents like I talk about grabbing some dinner!"

JJ was stunned. "What's wrong with that? I thought you'd be excited. Don't you want to know who killed your daughter?"

"Of course I do!" By now Dr. Ben was standing up and waving his tea mug around. "But not at the expense of hundreds of people... including you! Didn't you think this through at all? Are you going to inform the police of your plans? That you're actually hoping a deranged psychotic will appear that night so you can capture him in some kind of great heroic moment?"

"That's not what I want!" Now JJ stood as well, wondering how many confrontations he could have in one evening. At least he didn't feel like he had to be as calm as he had with Darryl. Dr. Ben sure wasn't calm. "I just want to find the guy!" he yelled. "I have to! It's the only way to break this fucking cycle! I have to find him. The police aren't catching him, and I'm going to keep having these dreams until I die, and *it's the only way to fix everything.*" JJ finished his speech by throwing his hands out by his sides and glaring at Dr. Ben.

"JJ!" Dr. Ben wasn't quite yelling, but his voice was definitely louder than it had been. "Is that really what you believe? That your happiness is entirely predicated on knowing who set that fire? Even if that was true, which it isn't, do you realize just how dangerous that line of thinking is? Just consider the people attending this benefit. If these people ever thought that this event was designed specifically to catch a murderer, do you think they'd be attending? Of course not! They'd be afraid for their lives. Does McKinley's mother even know what you're hoping will happen at this party?"

"Does it matter? Isn't there always a chance the guy who started the fire would show up, whether I think he might or not? Anybody could show up at this thing. I'm not asking him to come. I'm just *hoping* he will. He *has to come.*" JJ finished that sentence and charged up the basement stairs out of the den, planning to find his clothes and get the hell out of Dr. Ben's house.

Dr. Ben didn't follow him to the bathroom on the second floor, so JJ was surprised to find him waiting in the living room when JJ came storming downstairs. "Wait a second, JJ." Dr. Ben sighed, putting his hand up. "Just hear me out before you go."

JJ waited.

"You're right."

He was?

"This guy could show up no matter what. It doesn't matter whether you want him to or not. The problem is, JJ, that you *want* him to. You want him to appear at this event. You want these people to be in danger. You want to put yourself in danger."

JJ considered this. "I don't want to put other people in danger," he muttered into his only partially dried T-shirt.

"No? Just yourself, then?"

"If it means I get to catch the guy… I guess I think it's worth it."

Dr. Ben sank into the sofa he was standing in front of, but JJ stayed standing. He wasn't exactly planning on staying. "Is it worth your life to catch this guy?" Dr. Ben asked.

"Of course." JJ was incredulous again. "Don't you get it? I thought you, of all people, would get it. Wouldn't you die to find the guy who killed your daughter?"

Dr. Ben gave a harsh, dark laugh. "JJ, I spent the first three years after Sara died fairly suicidal. I would have given anything to catch the guy, to have her back—to have my life back."

He stood again. "Then I realized that it didn't matter if that man was ever caught. I was never going to have Sara back, and it didn't matter whether or not I lived or died. She was dead. That was all there was to it. I could spend the rest of my life living for her, trying to do good here and there in her name, or I could fall into a hole as black as the life of the man who killed her.

"So let me ask you, JJ: where are you in that equation? Do you still think finding this man will somehow change what happened to your parents? Do you think they'd want you to give your life for this man? This man who means nothing?"

"You don't get it." JJ was surprised by how quiet and broken his voice sounded. "It is worth it. I'm still having that dream, Dr. Ben. It's not going away. I just had it again, like, two nights ago. And every single time, it's like I'm reliving that day over and over again... over and over. I see everything. I see that bathroom, and that tattoo, and the fire next to me. It's like I'm never going to be allowed to forget that if I just hadn't wanted to go to the bathroom by myself, none of this would have happened."

"What do you mean?" Dr. Ben asked gently.

"I wanted to go to the bathroom by myself. I wanted to prove to them I could; that I was old enough. I was only in kindergarten, but I wanted to be all independent. I was so proud that they left my little sister with a sitter that day and took me to the movies. It was supposed to be a reward because I was such a great older brother and such a big boy." JJ shook his head. "I wasn't. I was so jealous of her. I wanted my parents all to myself again. I had them, that day. But I had to go and prove that I could take care of myself, 'cause I was supposed to be so grown up now."

"JJ, you going to the bathroom isn't the reason they died."

JJ was on the verge of angry, defiant tears now. "It is, don't you get it? If they had come, they wouldn't have been in the theater. They would have been with me. You would have saved all of us. They would have survived!"

It was silent for several long moments while JJ stared at the door, sucking in long deep breaths and blinking tears out of his eyes. Then Dr. Ben spoke.

"My daughter would have lived if I hadn't gotten popcorn."

"What?" JJ turned and gave all his attention back to Dr. Ben, who seemed to have sunk farther into the couch since JJ had last looked at him.

"There was a stampede… no one in the theater could get the door open because it had been jammed from the outside. Eventually some people got out, but in the chaos, my little eight-year-old didn't. If I'd been in the theater with her… if I hadn't gone to get us snacks… I could have gotten her out. I could have saved her. I never saw her again. All because I wanted popcorn."

JJ knew then why Dr. Ben didn't mind him invading his house and using his shower, and why he'd rescued him from the Pediatrics Ward that day, and even why he'd agreed to talk to JJ that very first afternoon in his office: it was easy to help the people who knew your worst pain before they'd even met you.

He sat down beside Dr. Ben on the couch.

"But JJ… it wasn't my fault. And it sure wasn't yours for using the john that day. Somebody murdered them. That's all there is to it. I know that now. It took me years. I don't want it to take you as long."

"And I do understand your desire to find this man. That doesn't mean you should put yourself—or others—in danger."

JJ didn't answer. It was something to think about.

"Another episode of *Scrubs* before you go?" Dr. Ben finally asked.

JJ looked around at the house and wondered if Maggie was even home yet. Probably not. "Sure, why not?"

Within another episode, they had come to an understanding.

Dr. Ben would consider coming to the benefit, and he wouldn't try to stop it from happening, on the condition that JJ allowed him to call Detective Starrow and suggest they have some personnel on hand. "They should anyway," Dr. Ben had said. "There is a very real chance this guy could return to the scene of his crime. You and McKinley were right about that. They should be prepared. Especially with the amount of people attending." He'd also made JJ promise not to do anything rash if he was able to identify Tattoo Man. "You get a cop," Dr. Ben had admonished.

JJ had agreed, knowing that if he saw the man with the tattoo, he wasn't going to be thinking all that straight.

He knew Dr. Ben was right: his parents wouldn't want him to put himself in danger.

But he wasn't making any guarantees.

CHAPTER 8

The Unbreakable Cycle

You can't break it
No one can

You're making it worse
Every time you look at me
I can't look away

How can—

"JJ?"

JJ slammed his notebook shut and looked up to find McKinley staring down at him.

"What are you doing here? Creative Writing started five minutes ago. Why are you writing in front of your locker instead of in class?"

"Uh…." JJ wasn't sure what to say. *I didn't want to see you because I was afraid you weren't speaking to me anymore, and I was afraid that I would be really upset to find out and I'm not sure what that would mean* didn't really seem like an appropriate answer. "Just didn't feel like going today. What are you doing here?"

"Teach sent me to find you. She wanted to make sure you were okay. Someone saw you out here."

"Oh." JJ didn't know what to say to that. Had Ms. Lyle made McKinley come, or had he volunteered?

McKinley sank down the bank of lockers to sit next to JJ. "I mean, I asked if I could come look for you. I was worried maybe you didn't come because of what happened in the library yesterday."

"Yeah?" JJ played with the cover of his writing notebook and risked a glance in McKinley's direction.

"Yeah. I mean, I know I said I'd be pissed if something happened to my tutoring."

"Are you?" JJ hoped his voice didn't sound as small as he thought it did.

"Nah." McKinley gave him a half smile, and liquor had never unwound the spring as quickly as that smile did. "I mean, I was a little upset at first. But Darryl believed me when I said I didn't know what was going on, and Penny didn't spill the beans. We're going to keep up the tutoring, so it's all good. Plus…." He paused, and JJ waited as his words hung in the air. "I was, like, impressed by how you handled that whole thing. Darryl can be such a bitch sometimes, and you really held your own with her."

"Yeah?" Now JJ felt himself smiling.

"Yeah." McKinley stood, reaching out a hand to pull JJ up too. "C'mon. If you hurry up, you can spend the next forty minutes in mysterious silence, pretending you're too good to share your stuff with the rest of us."

JJ rolled his eyes and followed obediently. McKinley was wearing a TV On The Radio T-shirt. One of JJ's favorite bands. Dr. Ben's words echoed in his head: *Who you like is who you like.*

He kept following.

"JJ, YOU can't wear that."

Not this again. "Why not?" JJ glanced over his outfit. He was wearing khakis and a polo shirt. Wasn't that what Maggie had wanted him to wear to his court appearance?

"This is semiformal, JJ. Some people will be in tuxes. You need to wear black pants, hon, and your white shirt… I'll go find you a tie."

JJ flinched. He didn't even know how a tie worked. "Are you sure, Maggie?"

She shook her head. "JJ, have you even noticed how I'm dressed?"

She was wearing a long blue dress and high heels. She'd even pulled up her strawberry blonde hair into some kind of complicated-looking hairdo. JJ had to admit she looked great.

"Fine," he grumbled. "Find me a tie."

He found the black pants and was trying to shake some wrinkles out of his white button-up shirt (which he'd found in a pile of clothes on the bottom of his closet), when Maggie came in.

"Oh, give me that to iron," she sighed as she tossed JJ something silvery. "See what you think of that. It was your dad's."

The tie was nice. It was striped with silver, gray, and black. JJ didn't have much of a fashion sense, but he thought it would look pretty good with the black pants. He bent over it to figure out how this was supposed to go around his neck, and he immediately breathed in a familiar scent: Tide and Old Spice. His father used to smell like Tide and Old Spice.

Before Maggie could come back to his room with the newly ironed shirt, JJ buried his nose in the tie for a few long moments.

I hope I make you proud tonight, Dad.

THE FRONT lobby of the Bijou Street Movie Theater was covered in white lights. It was a small lobby, and JJ had been wondering how McKinley's mother was going to fit an entire party into it.

But the party wasn't just in the lobby. It was spread throughout the entire theater, with a buffet in Theater One, a silent auction in Theater Two, and a showing of a short documentary commemorating the night of the fire in Theater Three. People were mingling through the lobby between the three theaters, stopping to take food from the well-dressed waitstaff circulating in the crowd.

JJ and Maggie stopped at what was normally the ticket counter, where someone greeted them and checked their names off a list. Nobody asked them for any money, but JJ had a feeling (based on the outfits people were wearing) that many of them were paying a lot to attend.

Maggie took something that looked like a mushroom off a waiter's tray and smiled at JJ. "I was a little apprehensive about coming tonight, JJ. I hope we can enjoy it."

JJ nodded. He knew Maggie had been surprised he'd wanted to go to the benefit at all. He still hadn't said anything to her about McKinley and their part in planning this.

"Do you think... do you think Penny will come?" JJ already knew the answer to that question even as he asked it.

Maggie smiled wryly. "I imagine Darryl will. However, I don't think she'll bring Penny, JJ. She knows you're coming, and she's more upset with you than ever right now." Maggie accepted a glass of champagne from another tray and went on. "At this point, I'm not sure when either of us will see Penny next."

"Maggie, I really didn't mean to make Darryl that mad."

Maggie eyed him over her champagne. "Really?"

"I mean, I was just at the library and—"

"JJ, don't give me that. I know you probably found out about Penny's tutoring. You knew exactly what you were doing."

JJ was surprised to see that Maggie was smiling a little.

"You're not mad?"

She sighed. "I suppose I should be, but I'm not. She's your sister, and Darryl and I have never seen eye to eye on this issue. I'm just glad you held your temper in check and didn't throw a punch at her."

"Nope. Just thought about it." JJ grinned.

Maggie squeezed his shoulder. "Let's not worry about it tonight, okay, JJ? Tonight I want to think about my brother and his wife... about how much I loved them. I want to think about them before the fire, not all the bad things that have come since. That's why I agreed to come."

"Okay," JJ murmured, wondering where he rated on that list of bad things.

They ate food from the buffet in Theater One. It was strange to eat fancy food like glazed duck in movie theater seats while classical music played in the background, but JJ kind of liked it. The food was good, and they ended up sitting next to an elderly couple who were actually pretty interesting.

"We used to come to these things all the time," said the woman, Mrs. Somersville. She was wearing some kind of fur getup wrapped around the shoulders of a sparkling red dress. JJ couldn't figure out if it was real. "There aren't enough charities and events in this tiny little town… especially ones I can wear my good furs to."

So they were real.

Her husband chuckled. "You'll have to forgive my wife. She hasn't quite forgiven me for moving her away from Boston to such a small town to run the new branch of my company. She wishes there were more to do here."

"Can you blame me?" Mrs. Somersville gestured to her surroundings. "I'm excited about attending a charity event in a movie theater, for goodness' sake!"

JJ had no idea older people could be funny.

"What brings you two out tonight?" Mr. Somersville asked. "I wouldn't have thought a teenager would be interested in attending an event like this.

Maggie squeezed JJ's shoulder. "We lost some family in the fire. We're here to honor them."

The couple got quiet very quickly. "Our apologies," murmured Mr. Somersville. "Perhaps we should leave the two of you be?"

"Of course not!" Maggie was indignant. "We're here to celebrate their memory tonight, not to mourn. JJ and I have already decided that. What do you do for a living, Mr. Somersville?"

He started going on about something having to do with insurance, and JJ returned to the task he'd been working on periodically throughout the evening: examining the right hand of every person he saw.

So far, no luck. Not a tattoo in sight. He did another scan of the theater. It was too difficult to see the people on the far end up close, so he excused himself to return to the buffet for more food. He managed to walk all around the theater on his way back to his seat, hoping that Maggie wouldn't notice. She was still engrossed in talking to the Somersvilles when JJ returned, and he hadn't seen a single hand with a tattoo.

Could he have had it removed? Could he be hiding somewhere? Thoughts were churning through JJ's head as he and Maggie left Theater One.

"What wonderful people!" Maggie was gushing. "And they took my card for the next time they need a photographer at one of their parties. If I can drum up a little business tonight...."

JJ wasn't really listening.

They walked through the silent auction in Theater Two. There was nothing there JJ could afford, let alone anything that looked very interesting. There was a trip for two to Paris, a spa day (what was a spa day?), some kind of small boat, a skiing vacation. JJ concentrated on people's hands.

Maggie was talking to some people whose wedding she'd photographed, and JJ was standing in front of a membership to the local history museum, wondering how much people would actually bid to get into a museum that had a total of five rooms, when someone tapped him on the shoulder.

"Jacob Jasper Jones," said Detective Starrow.

"Uh," replied JJ. For one thing, it took him a solid minute to recognize her. She was wearing a long black dress and silver jewelry instead of the suit she'd been wearing when they'd met. "You're here," he finally mumbled.

"Sure am. How are you doing?"

"Dr. Ben called you," JJ answered.

She laughed. "He didn't really need to. *Of course* we were going to have officers all over something like this—if ever someone like the arsonist was going to come out of hiding, this would be the place to do it." She winked. "But based on what Dr. Ben told me, I suspect you already knew that."

JJ didn't answer. Detective Starrow just kept smiling.

"For the record, I'm glad your friend suggested someone do this. This needed to be remembered on the ten-year mark."

JJ blinked. "Really? You don't think we were putting everyone in danger or something?"

The detective huffed a little. "JJ, I have this place so lit up with cops—undercover and uniformed—that if that asshole *does* show up or try something, he'll be in a jail cell before he can even pull a bottle of turpentine out of his pocket. But, for the record, the next time you try to go all MacGyver on this case, get in touch with me first, okay? I'd prefer to actually know when someone's holding a staging for my investigation. Makes staffing the thing a lot easier."

"Uh," JJ said again.

"Anyhoo, be safe tonight, kid. No chasing tattoos all by yourself." She left to talk to someone else, and JJ decided he should probably find Maggie and ask her if they could go back to the lobby. He didn't want to risk having another conversation with Detective Starrow where all he could say was "Uh."

"JJ!" McKinley waved to him from across the room as soon as JJ and Maggie stepped out of Theater Two, and JJ felt his heart beat a little faster. He started straightening his tie, and then stopped as soon as he realized he was doing it.

McKinley made it over to him quickly and pulled JJ in for one of those one-armed guy hugs some people did. JJ was so startled he couldn't figure out whether or not he liked it.

JJ pulled himself together long enough to do introductions. "McKinley, this is my Aunt Maggie. Maggie, this is McKinley. He's Penny's tutor."

"Oh!" Maggie put down her drink and shook McKinley's hand enthusiastically. "It's wonderful to meet you!"

They started talking about Penny and what a great kid she was, and JJ tried not to stare at McKinley. He had ditched his usual T-shirts and jeans for a dark blue suit, and JJ thought he looked... well, really good. He tried to channel Dr. Ben's words to stem any panic that thought raised.

Pretty soon Maggie wandered off to say hello to someone, leaving JJ and McKinley alone. "Have you seen Darryl?" JJ asked.

"Darryl's here with some of her family, but she didn't bring Penny. She's still mad at you, I guess. So, have you had any luck with... you know?"

"No, nothing yet."

McKinley nodded. "Well, I'm keeping my eyes out too. You know the police are here, right?"

"Yeah." JJ tried to shake off the memory of how stupid he'd just looked in front of Detective Starrow. "If you do see anyone, we should let them know right away."

"Really? I guess I sort of had this image of you wanting to get to the guy first."

"I do." JJ shrugged. "But there are other people here... you know. We should make sure they're safe."

McKinley shook his head. "You never stop surprising me, Jones." He took a sip of his soda. "Anyway, you and your aunt should check out the film in Theater Three. My mom has a friend who made it just for tonight. It's a memorial documentary. Your parents should be in it, JJ." He frowned slightly as he finished speaking.

That hadn't occurred to JJ. His stomach twisted a little.

JJ did a few more laps around the event, keeping an eye out for tattoos. Eventually Maggie found him again, and she asked if he wanted to see the movie in Theater Three.

And for some reason, JJ said yes.

At the beginning of the hall that led down to Theater Three, JJ suddenly stopped. "You okay, JJ?" Maggie whispered.

JJ nodded. For years he'd refused to even come into the Bijou Street Movie Theater. But when JJ was about ten, he'd decided he didn't want to turn down his friends' invitations to birthday parties and hangout sessions anymore. So he'd asked Maggie to bring him to a movie in this exact theater. He had made it through the whole thing by clutching Maggie's hand and hoping no one saw.

It had been a success, though. After all, it wasn't really Theater Three itself that terrified JJ: he hadn't even been there during the fire. It was the theater restroom. JJ hadn't set foot in that room since he was five. He had no plans to anytime soon.

"Let's just get to the theater," he said. Maggie nodded, needing no explanation, and they walked swiftly down the hall to the door on the end.

Inside, the theater was lowly lit and quiet. People spoke in whispered tones, and a countdown on the theater screen announced that the next showing of the documentary would begin in one minute. He and Maggie found a seat in the middle of the theater just as the lights dimmed, and the movie began.

At first, JJ was so tense he barely noticed he was gripping the armrests of his seat. The narrator began with the date of the infamous fire. He talked about the movies playing that day, and the documentary showed footage of what the theater had looked like ten years ago.

Of course, it looked almost identical now. After the fire, the owners had insisted that it be restored exactly as it had been. JJ had always had mixed feelings about that choice. Sometimes he wished that when he walked into the Bijou Street Movie Theater, it felt like a completely different place than it had the day his parents died.

On screen, the documentary addressed the nature of the arsonist: what he had done, where. The turpentine that had been found in Theater Three. The chair that had been used to jam the emergency exit.

They didn't show any direct images of the fire itself, and JJ was really glad they didn't. He would've had to leave the show; he just knew it.

Then the tone of the documentary changed. The music slowly switched from something with a deep and intense beat to something with a lot of violins and a slow, classic feeling. Pictures of people began flashing across the screen, each with two dates below them.

It took JJ a few moments to realize that these were the victims of the fire. Next to him, Maggie squeezed his shoulder again.

It was several long moments before a picture of JJ's parents, hugging and smiling, appeared on the screen. JJ remembered it from the funeral. On the screen flashed the words, "Marilyn Rachel Jones, 1974-2003, and Jasper Franklin Jones, 1972-2003."

More pictures flashed, over and over again in rapid succession, but all JJ saw was that picture. His father's eyes filled with happiness. His mother's bright smile.

Then the documentary was over, and the light was coming up in Theater Three. JJ stumbled out of the row of seats, heading for the door, and Maggie followed him. He could hear her sniffling a little, but he didn't look at her as they spilled out the door of the theater and back into the bright lights of the lobby.

"Well, if it isn't JJ Jones. Split any femoral arteries lately?"

JJ looked to his right and found Dr. Ben standing there. He smiled.

JJ SPENT the next forty-five minutes in the lobby with Dr. Ben and Maggie, eating at least eight of some kind of tiny chocolate dessert and wishing he could join them in downing some champagne. Dr. Ben said he had no desire to see the film. "Don't get me wrong, I admire you two for checking it out," he said. "But if I wanted to sob in front of complete strangers, I'd just start chopping an onion on the ticket counter. Besides, I haven't been in that particular theater in years."

No one asked how many.

Dr. Ben and Aunt Maggie discussed the economy, the housing market, and health insurance—everything but the fire. JJ ignored them and watched hands, his heart sinking a little more every time a blank one went by.

Dr. Ben and Maggie were deep into a discussion about Maggie's photography business when Darryl came gliding out of Theater Two and over to them.

She looked as intimidating as ever, in a dark black dress and black stiletto heels.

"Well, Maggie! I'm so glad you made it." She reached over to kiss Maggie's cheek. "Who's this?"

"This is Dr. Benjamin Peragena. He's... ah... JJ's new pediatrician." JJ saw her lips twitch and knew she must not have told Darryl the story of the bloody breakfast.

"Good to meet you." Darryl shook Dr. Ben's hand and moved her gaze to JJ. "Nice to see you, JJ."

"You too, Darryl." JJ kept his tone as even as possible. "Is Penny here?"

"No." Darryl kept an impossibly fake smile plastered across her face. "Much too late for her, you know. So," she continued, "do you remember my brother, Lucas O'Dell? Lucas is in town visiting me for a few days."

For the first time, JJ noticed a tall, dark-haired man standing next to Darryl. He was wearing an expensive-looking suit and smiling broadly. The only thing marring his image was a bright white cast wrapped around his right hand and all the way down his wrist. JJ couldn't help but notice that Maggie was staring blatantly at him.

JJ frowned for a moment at the cast, then realized there wasn't much chance it was covering up the tattoo he was looking for, anyway. What were the odds that Darryl's *brother* was the arsonist?

"Good to see you all again," Lucas said. "I remember you both from when I used to help Darryl and... Marilyn at their store when it first opened." JJ noticed he had a difficult time saying his mother's name. "Marilyn and I were very close. I was hoping to be able to attend tonight, for her."

JJ stared hard, trying to place this man. He didn't look familiar at all. "You worked at the store? Why didn't I ever see you there?"

Lucas's smile turned wistful. "I mainly worked evening shifts; I was attending college at the time. You were almost never in the store that late."

McKinley suddenly appeared by JJ's side, as though he had been there the whole night. "Darryl. It's good to see you."

Darryl nodded. "You too, McKinley. Please pass along my compliments to your mother—she planned a lovely evening." She stirred her drink and studied McKinley, eyes narrowing a little. "I've been wondering how it was that your mother came to be the one planning this event?"

"Your mother planned all this?" Maggie asked.

McKinley didn't even blink before answering. "Oh, it's not a coincidence. I remembered what you'd told me about how Penny's parents died, and I started thinking about the fact that no one here in town really talks about the fire anymore. When I mentioned that to my mom, we realized it was the ten-year anniversary. She wanted to do something to make sure it didn't stay forgotten."

JJ tried to keep his jaw from dropping. Now *that* was impressive. The speech didn't even sound rehearsed.

Darryl nodded, satisfied. "Well, she did a lovely job. McKinley, have you met Lucas, Penny's uncle? He's visiting us."

"Great to meet ya."

"And I'm Dr. Ben, JJ's pediatrician." Dr. Ben's eyes wrinkled with amusement. He had definitely figured out that this was *the* McKinley—not that there were many McKinleys living in the area.

"Nice to meet you," McKinley said smoothly. "Actually, JJ, could you help me out with something for a minute? I need to move a table for my mom."

"Sure," said JJ, relieved to step out of the way of Darryl's boring eyes and Dr. Ben's laughing ones.

"Great. Thanks." As soon as they were away from Darryl, McKinley began whispering. "The benefit ends soon; everyone's going to be leaving. I haven't seen any sign of Tattoo Man yet, have you?"

"No. And I think I've seen every wrist in this place. Well, except for Lucas's, since he's got that cast on. But he knew my mom; there's no way it was him."

"Well, I thought we should do a last round. I'll go look through the theaters again. You do the men's room, okay?"

JJ froze in place, a few feet from the door to Theater One. "What?"

"Well, you never know, right? The theaters should be empty now, but I'll double check. And the bathroom always just seems like a good place to hide."

It sure does, thought JJ.

"Anyway, be back in a minute." McKinley was gone before JJ could even respond.

JJ dragged himself to the entrance of the men's room. The door was exactly the same as it was in his memory.

He stood there, amidst the scattered people who walked around him to use the restroom, ignoring their murmurs of how rude he was.

He thought about cycles, and fires, and turpentine, and dreams, and McKinley leading him to this doorway. Then he walked inside.

The inside was also exactly how he remembered it: A row of three sinks off to the left. Two toilet stalls, with two urinals on their far right. The spot on the floor where toilet paper had been stacked, ready to be placed into stalls after the theater closed.

He moved off to the side, breathing hard, and watched four or five men cycle through the bathrooms and sinks. All of their hands were blank. They left, and JJ stood there, shaking.

"JJ?" McKinley poked his head into the door. "What's taking so long?" He stepped inside when he saw JJ, pale and propping himself up against a stall door. "Are you okay? Did you see him?" he asked excitedly.

"There's no one here," JJ whispered.

"Oh."

"I mean, *there's no one here,*" JJ repeated.

McKinley grimaced. "Oh shit. I totally forgot about you and this bathroom." He grabbed JJ and pushed him into the handicap stall, where he locked the door behind them, shoved JJ down onto the seat, and pushed his head between his legs. "JJ, I'm so fucking sorry. I never should have sent you in here. Are you okay?"

JJ laughed, pushing McKinley's arms off his shoulders before grabbing them and using them to pull himself up. "No, you don't understand. There's no one here, McKinley! No one! I stood in this bathroom, and I'm still here, and everything's fine. I can do it. I can be in the bathroom and…." He stopped, suddenly realizing how stupid the whole thing sounded when he tried to explain it.

But McKinley just smiled. "Yeah? You're okay?"

"Yeah." JJ blinked.

"Good." McKinley reached out to give him a hug—not a bro hug this time, but a real hug—and when he pulled away, JJ didn't let go completely.

Instead, JJ reached up and pushed his lips to McKinley's.

The kiss started light and slow, and a low tingle built itself inside JJ, moving within him as he and McKinley pressed their lips tighter together, and JJ moved more solidly into McKinley's body. JJ knew right then that Dr. Ben was right: you are who you are.

When they finally pulled apart, McKinley cocked an eyebrow at JJ. "Not gay, huh?"

JJ shrugged. "Someone told me not to think about the labels so much."

ON THE drive home, all Maggie could talk about was Lucas. "I can't believe how much he's changed! We didn't know each other well, of course. I really only remember him from Jasper and Marilyn's wedding and a few other events. I didn't even know he helped with the store that much. He always had a handsome face, but it was so sad. He often looked so unhappy. He seems so much more together these days. He's an artist, you know, a painter. He's had shows in New York and New Haven and Boston…. He came back into town just for this benefit, but now that he's back, he's going to stay for a while and try to arrange some shows for art galleries in the Burlington area…."

JJ barely heard her. He was too busy wondering about Tattoo Man, who'd never showed up that evening. And the kiss. His first kiss. His first kiss with a guy. No, his first kiss with *McKinley.*

Maggie was still going on as they pulled into the driveway. "Of course, he's taking some time from painting right now. He broke his wrist last week, so he says it's difficult right now…."

"Wait." Suddenly JJ was paying attention again. "You said he's a painter?"

Maggie laughed. "Where have you been? I've been talking about his painting for the last five minutes." She went on about Lucas's painting awards, but JJ stopped listening again. Lucas was a *painter.* Maybe, JJ thought, he shouldn't have been so quick to stop wondering what was under that cast.

JJ shook his head as he stepped out of the car. He was getting so paranoid that he was starting to think someone might get a cast just to hide a tattoo.

THE NEXT day, JJ was checking out of the physical therapy wing in the hospital after his usual shift. He'd just hung his volunteer's jacket up along with the others and was writing the time on the sign-out list when he saw Jeremy standing at the other end of the check-in desk, dressed in scrubs. Had Dr. Ben mentioned that Jeremy was a doctor too? JJ couldn't remember.

JJ ambled over. "Jeremy?" He hoped it was okay to call him that.

Jeremy looked up from the clipboard. "Hello. Aren't you the kid from Ben's house?" He wasn't smiling, but he didn't look unhappy either.

"Yeah. I just wanted to thank you for being so nice that night and all. I'm sorry about showing up like that all randomly."

He shrugged. "No worries. I was just there using some of Ben's exercise equipment. It wasn't a big deal."

"Great." JJ hesitated, and Jeremy looked curiously at him, as if to say, *what else?*

"I didn't see you at the benefit for the Bijou Street Movie Theater fire the other night." JJ wasn't sure why he said that. Probably because he was still curious whether or not this was *the* ex, the one that Ben had broken up with after his daughter died.

The way Jeremy's face hardened made it pretty clear this was the same ex. "I'm sorry, JJ, but I barely know you. Why would you bring that up?"

JJ squirmed. "I'm sorry… I mean, I said that because I was there. I mean, I um, lost some people in that fire. Dr. Ben told me about, you know, his daughter. I'm really sorry, you know, if that was your daughter too." JJ knew he was barely making sense and talking almost a million miles a minute, and he wished he'd just stuck to his original thank you.

"Oh." Jeremy's face was like stone now. "Well… my sympathies to you as well. I have patients to go see." He turned to go.

"Yeah. Dr. Ben didn't mention you were a doctor too."

"I'm one of the physical therapists here, actually. Speaking of which, what are you doing in the physical therapy wing?"

"Ah, I volunteer here." JJ decided not to mention that his volunteer time was mandated by the court system.

"I see." Jeremy was studying him again. "Good for you. I'll probably see you around then."

JJ was leaving the hospital, wondering if he should add that conversation to the list of the mistakes he'd made in his life, when he noticed Darryl standing outside at the curb.

"Hello, JJ." She wrapped a scarf tighter around her neck. "I'd like to talk to you. I spoke to Maggie this afternoon, and she said you'd be finishing your shift of community service about now. I offered to drive you home for her."

Woo-hoo. He'd have to thank Maggie later.

They were barely out of the driveway of the hospital, though, when JJ understood why Maggie had wanted him to talk to Darryl. "JJ, I need to talk to you about Penny," Darryl began. "She's unhappy with me lately."

JJ was pretty proud that he held in the sarcastic comment about Penny finally joining the club.

"She's been angry about not being able to see you. She's also angry I kept her home from the benefit last night. She's not been herself at all lately… very sullen all the time. She was especially upset over the library scene; she said it wasn't fair that she should get in trouble for saying hello to you. Actually, she didn't so much say it as scream it at me."

JJ coughed to cover the laugh that almost escaped him.

"I realize you and I have had our issues over the years, JJ. I have tried to do what is best for Penny, but maybe I have been a little overzealous about keeping you away from her. Maggie says you're doing very well with your community service, and that your grades are even up lately."

Were they? JJ hadn't even noticed.

"I was thinking that you and Maggie might come to my house for Thanksgiving in a few weeks. I think it would make Penny happy."

"Really?" JJ wondered if Darryl was playing some kind of sick game with him.

"Really. JJ, I can't truly apologize for what has happened between you and me over the years. As I said before, I only did what I thought was right for Penny. Clearly, though, I overstepped recently. I do apologize for that."

JJ thought she had overstepped years ago, but right then didn't seem to be the best time to say something.

"So, will you join us for Thanksgiving?"

"Sure." Normally, Thanksgiving wasn't high on JJ's list of favorite holidays. He and Maggie always went to her friend Janet's house, where there were tons of people, and he always ended up watching hours of football, which he wasn't really that interested in, and eating at the kids' table with Janet's boring nieces and nephews. This Thanksgiving was definitely looking up.

Of course, he'd have to see Patrick, but he'd worry about that later.

"Excellent. I'll tell Penny. I can trust you and Patrick to stay away from each other?" Apparently Darryl wasn't waiting to worry about that.

"Sure. No big deal. I mean, we do go to the same school and everything. We're fine." That was a little bit of an exaggeration. Patrick and JJ avoided all contact with each other at school. JJ had even switched out of class once just because Patrick was in it. Whenever they did end up in the same space, Patrick was always pretty hostile.

JJ was getting out of the car at his house when Darryl added something. "JJ…. Penny said she enjoyed seeing you at the library. If McKinley says you're not an interference, I won't object if you want to help Penny with her tutoring sessions in the future." She sounded very begrudging, but JJ didn't really care. It was as if everything he wanted was suddenly falling into his lap. Who was he to question that?

He was still grinning when he walked into the house. Maggie looked up from the stove, where she was making dinner. "Huh. Betcha never thought you'd be that happy to see Darryl, did you?"

CHAPTER 9

BON IVER'S "Skinny Love" filled McKinley's bedroom, and JJ sank into the music. Justin Vernon's voice usually lured him into kind of a trance anyway, and this particular song always got to him. Especially the part about being patient. And fine. And kind.

"You have excellent taste in music," JJ said as the song ended, and McKinley laughed.

They'd been doing this a lot since the night of the benefit—just sitting on McKinley's bedroom floor, going through his iTunes library together. Sometimes they talked, sometimes they made out, but they hadn't done much of anything more than that. Mostly, they just listened to music. It turned out JJ had been right, and McKinley's T-shirts were proof that he and JJ had musical taste in common.

"It's a great song." McKinley leaned back against the bed and clicked something on the computer that caused "Skinny Love" to start moving through the speakers again. "I think about the lyrics of this song a lot."

"Yeah?" JJ wasn't really that surprised. The more he learned about McKinley, the more he realized how much they thought alike.

"Yeah. What do you think it's about?"

JJ didn't even have to consider the question before answering. "I know what it's about. It's about disappointment. And starting over. And wondering what you could have done differently."

McKinley pulled JJ closer, until JJ was pressed up against him instead of the bed. Poses like this were still new to JJ, but it felt good, and he found himself relaxing into it rather than resisting. McKinley rested his chin on top of JJ's head. "Wow. You think?"

"I know. The way the guitar melds into the lyrics... the guy's regretful. But those chords on the end, the way they move up... it's like he knows there's still something else, but he's sad this ended the way it did. That things didn't go differently."

They sat in silence, listening to the rest of the song play out. "Last Train" by Travis came on before McKinley spoke again. "JJ, why do you drink so much?"

JJ pulled away from McKinley fast. "What are you talking about?" He'd been avoiding drinking near McKinley ever since the night McKinley'd brought him home from the kegger.

McKinley shrugged. "People talk, JJ. They say you get really drunk at every party you go to. And I'm pretty sure you've been avoiding partying with me since we started hanging out, but I'm also pretty sure you're still drinking a lot."

JJ's eyes narrowed. "What the fuck makes you think that?"

McKinley's eyes didn't narrow back, but his voice wasn't soft, either. "Like I said, people talk. And they say you're still showing up at places with Lewis."

JJ stood up so that he was looking down at McKinley. "What's it to you? So I like having a good time. What you are, my keeper?"

McKinley crossed his arms but stayed sitting. "No. But to be honest, I thought maybe I was your boyfriend. Or was about to be. So I think I have a right to ask."

JJ opened his mouth and closed it several times before any sound came out. "McKinley... I mean, you're the first guy I ever kissed. First *person* I've ever kissed."

McKinley rolled his eyes. "JJ, I know that. And for the record, I think you've handled all this self-discovery pretty well. I'm not asking you to out yourself to the school. If you don't want to date me exclusively right now, I get that. But if you'd like to, I'd like that too. Either way, I care about you. I want to make sure you're okay. And people say you and Lewis are still going out a lot, and I know you're avoiding ending up at the same parties as me, so I started to wonder why you're getting hammered so much and why you don't want me to see it."

"I have to go." JJ found his coat on the floor and got to the doorway as fast as he could.

"What the hell? You're bailing? Just because I asked you about the partying?" McKinley stood up, clearly pissed.

"Yeah, I'm bailing." JJ practically snarled as he said it. "Look, you know how I am about sharing shit, okay? I've shared a ton of shit with you, and I get to decide what I share. You want to get all up in my business about what my friends and I do for fun? Screw that. I don't tell you what to do."

"JJ, I'm not telling you what to do, I'm just asking—"

"Asking me why I'm a drunk," JJ said sarcastically. "Yeah. I got that. Well, listen to people all you want, McKinley. They probably talk a lot about how I keep failing gym class, too. Ya wanna talk about that? Go ahead and ask me. Just try."

McKinley looked stunned. "What *is* your problem, man? I thought we were getting closer, but you're acting like the same silent little shit from Creative Writing right now. We've been hanging out almost every afternoon since you kissed me—yeah, you kissed *me*, remember—and you won't even talk to me about why you party? And you're pissed because I even asked? Screw that." He opened the door to his bedroom. "Don't let the door smack your maybe-gay ass on the way out, then."

JJ didn't, but he did slam the door behind him.

He checked his cell phone a few times as he practically ran back to his house, half expecting McKinley to text him an apology. But McKinley never did.

That night it took a third of a bottle of Wild Turkey, stolen from Lewis's father's stash, to uncoil the spring.

THE NEXT day was the day before Thanksgiving, so after JJ finished his shift in the physical therapy wing, he went up to Dr. Ben's office to see how he was spending the holiday.

Dr. Ben was finishing up paperwork when JJ came in. "Hey there!"

"Hey." JJ settled into one the chairs in the office. "I just came to say happy Thanksgiving."

"To you, as well. Doing anything special?"

"Yeah, for once. Darryl invited me and Maggie over. She says Penny's been real unhappy about not seeing me." JJ shrugged. "What are you doing?"

"Oh, not much. My sister and brother-in-law invited me to their home in upstate New York. I may go; I may just stay home and watch football.

JJ winced at the image of Dr. Ben sitting alone in that big, empty house on Thanksgiving. "You should go to your sister's, Dr. Ben. Or, maybe," he added, suddenly feeling mischievous, "you could have Thanksgiving with Jeremy."

"Excuse me?" Dr. Ben chortled. "Where did that come from?"

"Oh, you know. I see him sometimes down in Physical Therapy. He looks, I don't know, lonely." That was definitely true. JJ actually ran into Jeremy pretty often now that he was doing more and more hours in Physical Therapy, trying to finish his community service as soon as possible. They never had a real conversation, but Jeremy always said "Hi" when JJ did. He did look lonely. Almost all the time.

"I see. JJ, you do realize that Jeremy and I aren't together anymore?" Dr. Ben looked almost amused by the conversation they were having.

"Sure. But you still like him, right?"

"JJ, that's none of your business."

"I know." JJ sighed. "I just don't think you should be alone on Thanksgiving."

"Thanks for the advice. I'll try to visit my sister. You, in the meantime, should enjoy the time you have with your sister."

"Yeah." JJ got up and paced the office for a minute, looking at the diplomas lining Dr. Ben's walls. "Dr. Ben, can I ask you a question?"

"Of course, JJ." Dr. Ben put down the pen in his hand and studied JJ intently.

"You know how McKinley and I are sort of together now?

"Yes." Dr. Ben was the only person JJ had told about kissing McKinley the night of the benefit.

"Ummm... what do you do if you want to make up with someone but you don't think you did anything wrong, and they think you did?"

Dr. Ben made a sound like he was trying not to laugh. "You and McKinley have a fight, JJ?"

"Yeah." JJ ran his hands through his hair and sat back down again. "He asked me about some stuff I didn't want to talk about. I got pissed at him for asking. He got pissed at me for getting pissed. He hasn't texted me or spoken to me since."

"JJ, if anyone gets not wanting to talk about things, it's me."

JJ nodded. He supposed Dr. Ben was right about that.

"That's one of the reasons Jeremy and I aren't together anymore, you know. After Sara passed, I stopped talking to him. He wanted to work through things, so that we could be there for each other. I kept turning him away. I didn't want to deal with any of it."

"So were you wrong? Or was he? Trying to get you to talk about stuff you didn't want to talk about?" JJ shuffled his feet as he waited for an answer.

Dr. Ben shook his head. "JJ, relationships aren't usually about right and wrong. It's a lot more complicated than that. But I do regret not trying harder to talk to him. He loved me. I loved him. Maybe if I'd let him in a little more, we'd still be together. And really, what was wrong with him trying to get me, his partner, to talk to him about something that had horribly affected both of us?"

JJ sank back into the seat across from Ben. "I drink sometimes," he blurted out. "McKinley asked me about it."

Dr. Ben raised an eyebrow. "Ah."

"What should I do?"

Dr. Ben frowned. "JJ, I told you once that you should let yourself do what you want, and see what you figure out. Seems to me you want to let yourself do the right thing here, but you're not sure how." He reached into a desk drawer and pulled out a pamphlet, which he placed on the desk in front of JJ. "You should decide what to do, JJ. Do what you *want*, not what you're used to doing or what you think others expect you to do. Just like you did with McKinley in the first place."

The pamphlet was called "A Message to Teenagers: How to Tell When Drinking is Becoming a Problem."

IT WAS Patrick who answered the door at Darryl's house. JJ looked at him warily. He hoped this wasn't an omen.

"Oh. It's you." Patrick glared.

Next to JJ, Maggie smiled. "Hello, Patrick. It's nice to see you again. May we come in?"

Patrick turned abruptly, leaving the door wide open. JJ and Maggie stepped inside. "What an abhorrent child, still," Maggie whispered to JJ. "If I didn't know that he treated Penny like a princess...."

It was true, unfortunately. When he was younger, JJ had been on the constant lookout for signs that Patrick was treating Penny as badly as he treated JJ (and, JJ thought, most people), but Patrick was the perfect adoptive brother. He and Dennis both acted like Penny was a glass doll.

"You're here!" Penny threw herself into JJ's arms while he and Maggie were still standing in the foyer.

"Of course we're here!" Maggie took her turn at a hug and planted a large kiss on Penny's cheek. "We wouldn't miss it."

"Let's go!" Penny tugged on the sleeve of JJ's polo shirt, which Maggie had insisted he wear again. "Everyone's in the dining room; we were waiting for you."

Darryl's dining room was as huge as JJ remembered, and perfectly decorated for Thanksgiving, with fancy-looking tablecloths and place mats and large centerpieces spread out across the table.

"Good, you're here!" Darryl's husband, David, came over to shake JJ's hand and hug Maggie. "I'm so glad you made it."

JJ couldn't help but smile back at him. David had almost always been the one to come and wake JJ out of a nightmare when he had lived with them. The night of the fight, after Darryl had pulled JJ off of

Patrick and rushed Patrick away to the emergency room, David had found an icepack for JJ's black eye and held him on the couch for what seemed like hours, while JJ sobbed and sobbed, refusing to explain what had happened. To this day, JJ remembered a time later that night, when he had heard David standing up for him, trying to convince Darryl that she was overreacting. It hadn't worked, but JJ had remained forever grateful to David for trying.

"Have a seat—I think there are two by Lucas."

Maggie's face lit up. "Lucas is here?"

"Sure; he's staying with us until Christmas." David pointed through the crowd of people gathered around the table to two seats at the other end. "Half of Darryl's family is here today, I think, and a good chunk of mine. Penny is sitting near Lucas too." JJ thought David winked at him when he said that, but he couldn't be sure.

They ended up sitting right in between Penny and Lucas, with JJ next to Penny and Maggie next to Lucas. JJ thought that both he and Maggie had never been so excited about a Thanksgiving dinner. He tried not to gape while Maggie blushed and laughed at everything Lucas said to her. He knew Maggie dated a little, but she almost never brought anyone home. JJ had actually never seen his aunt flirt. It was weird.

Penny was telling JJ about how well she was doing at school because of tutoring, and how much better her teacher said her reading was, when David came out of the kitchen with a turkey as big as Maggie's microwave. "Time to eat!" he announced.

"Denny, would you say grace?" Darryl and David finished placing side dishes on the table and sat down. Darryl gestured at Dennis. JJ had been trying to avoid making eye contact with Dennis. Patrick was sitting right next to him, and making accidental eye contact with Patrick could only mean trouble.

"Sure, Ma. Ah…. God, thanks for bringing family and friends together… especially family we haven't been able to see for such a long time." JJ noticed Dennis give Lucas a long look as he said that. *Interesting.* "Thanks for all the delicious food, and thanks for letting us share it together. Amen."

Everyone echoed his amen, and as the food came around, JJ forgot about Dennis's comment—until dessert.

Lucas was passing the pumpkin pie to Maggie, who was laughing hysterically over something he had said, when the corner of the cast above the thumb caught on the pie dish. If JJ hadn't been so attuned to people's right hands, he probably wouldn't even have noticed. But as Lucas hurried to unhook the pie plate from his cast and grimaced like he was in pain, JJ knew exactly what he saw: a splash of color.

Of course, he didn't see a tattoo. It could have been anything: dirt, a shadow. It was the placement that caused JJ's eyes to narrow. The spot was exactly where the beginning of the arsonist's paintbrush would be.

JJ stared at Lucas's hand as Maggie laughed and cut pie. He took his piece, listened to Penny beg for the whipped cream, and tried to decide what to do. Finally, he spoke.

"Lucas, how did you hurt your hand?" He hoped his voice wasn't shaking.

Lucas glanced down at the cast. "Oh, it was silly. I was helping a friend move some furniture. I slipped and broke it. I have to keep the cast for a few more weeks."

Maggie looked up from her pie. "That must be ruining your career plans right now."

Lucas nodded. "At least it's been a good excuse to hang out in Vermont for a while and work on getting some new shows up here. Still, I'll be glad to lose the cast and get back to work."

"Bummer," JJ mumbled. "So, where have you been all these years, anyway?" he asked more loudly. "Denny said some of the family hadn't been around during grace."

Suddenly Patrick, from six seats away, was paying attention. "What does it matter to you, JJ?" he snarled.

JJ feigned innocence. "I was just curious. Wondered if he was doing any cool stuff for the art world." Patrick glared but went back to his pie, and Lucas answered.

"Nothing that interesting, JJ. Just traveling… here and there. The fire upset me greatly, you know. I considered your mother a great friend. I spent several years recovering from the horror of that night, just going from state to state looking for ways to make money painting."

Now JJ was annoyed. What did this guy know about it? He thought *he* had spent several years recovering from that night? Who did he think he was?

And then it made sense, like a light suddenly flipped on in a darkened room. Lucas had something on his hand in the right place, and he had spent "years recovering from the horror of that night."

It also made no sense. What could Lucas's motive possibly have been? But JJ thought for sure he had a suspect: Lucas, Darryl's younger brother and one of his mother's friends, was possibly the arsonist behind the Bijou Street Movie Theater Fire.

And he was eating pie two seats away from JJ.

CHAPTER 10

"I DID it... I did it," the man whispered. *"I finally did it."*

JJ moved to the sinks, more eager than ever to return to the comforting gaze of his mother. But the noise of his sneakers against the tile alerted the strange man to JJ's presence, and now the stranger was turning around to face him.

First JJ saw the blue jeans, the red long-sleeve shirt, and of course, the tattoo. But as JJ's gaze traveled upward, something strange happened: he also saw the man's face.

Emblazoned in JJ's mind, laughing at him with horribly crazed eyes, was Lucas.

JJ sat bolt upright in bed, that last image from the dream stamped firmly in his mind. He jumped off the bed and ran for the bathroom. Halfway through losing most of his Thanksgiving dinner, he was sorry he'd gone for the extra helping of mashed potatoes.

Back in his room a few minutes later, JJ checked the clock: 5:00 a.m. Too late to try and go back to sleep. Plenty of time to lie in bed and wonder if he should say something to Maggie about the possibility that Lucas was Tattoo Man.

He'd spent most of the ride home from dinner last night with his fists clenched in his lap while Maggie went on about how successful Lucas was, and how wonderful it was to see him again. He couldn't figure out how to say something without sounding like a crazy person.

After all, how did you accuse someone of mass murder on the evidence that they had a cast?

But then JJ's eyes caught one of the rare photos in his room. It was a framed photo Maggie had put on his dresser years ago. It was of the two of them with Penny, having a picnic in the park on an afternoon Darryl had let them spend together. It was one of the few pictures of JJ where he was actually smiling.

And JJ knew he was going to say something to Maggie. No matter how crazy it sounded.

"BUT WHAT if it *is* him? He's got a cast, Maggie!" JJ was ranting, stalking around his living room. Maggie was sitting calmly, trying to figure out what JJ was talking about. It was only nine o'clock in the morning, and she'd barely been out of bed for ten minutes when JJ had started in about Lucas and how dangerous he could be.

"Let me get this straight: you think *Lucas* burned down the Bijou?"

"I know, it sounds crazy. But I saw something under his cast! Maybe. And it's in the exact same place as the tattoo is on the guy from my dream! And he was talking about how he hadn't been able to see his family for years, and he said that he went away for a while after the fire because the night was so hard on him. And the last time I had the dream *I saw his face*, Maggie!" JJ stopped in the middle of the floor and waited for a response.

"JJ… you realize how absolutely ridiculous this sounds, right?" Maggie asked, still incredulous.

"Who else has a tattoo in that exact same place? Who else? It has to be him!"

"But you didn't even see a tattoo, JJ. What you saw could be anything. And of course your mind has added him to the dream; you've convinced yourself that he did it! Not to mention, JJ, that Lucas cared very much for your mother. Why would he burn down a theater she was in?"

JJ threw up his hands. "I don't know! Maybe it had nothing to do with her! Maybe he didn't even know she was there! All I know is that it could have been him." He sank into a chair next to her. "You think I'm crazy, don't you?"

Maggie leaned forward and took JJ's hands. "JJ... I know that ever since this dream appeared on the scene, it's probably been hard not to see tattoos everywhere. It makes sense. But kiddo, you don't even know for sure that you saw a tattoo under that cast. And you can't go around accusing every painter you meet of setting the Bijou on fire."

JJ gritted his teeth. "You like him, don't you?"

Maggie blushed. "He's an attractive man, JJ. Yes, if he asks me out, I'll probably say yes."

Now JJ leaned forward so he could clench her hands hard. "Then *please*, Mags. I have to be sure." He lowered his voice. "I can't lose you too."

Then JJ was being crushed in a hug, and he knew Maggie would help.

That afternoon, Maggie and JJ were ringing Darryl's doorbell.

"Yes?" She answered the door looking annoyed, wearing an old sweatshirt and spandex pants. JJ had a feeling they had caught her right in the middle of an exercise session.

Maggie's smile was so wide it looked unnatural. "Do you have a few moments, Darryl? JJ wanted to ask you something, and it seemed to me that it was a little too personal to ask over the phone."

Darryl glanced at her watch. "I suppose I could spare a few moments... I was about to leave for yoga." She gestured them into the house with a sweep of her arm and led them to her immaculate beige living room.

JJ sank into the same overstuffed couch he had sat on as a child. A sudden memory of crying into David's lap on that couch didn't do much for his confidence.

Maggie nodded at him to start, and he hoped his voice wasn't going to shake too much. It never stopped amazing him how tense Darryl made him. How his sweet and calming mother had ever been best friends with Darryl was beyond him.

"Well... so, Darryl, I've been remembering some things about the fire lately."

Darryl sighed. "This is about the fire?"

JJ nodded and hoped that she wouldn't keep interrupting him. It ruined his momentum. "Yeah—I mean, yes, it is. I've been having this dream, only I figured out that it's probably a memory of the arsonist, of seeing him in the bathroom that day. In my dream, he has a tattoo of a paintbrush on his hand."

Now what was he supposed to say? This was the part where he was supposed to accuse her brother of mass murder. As rude and blunt as JJ knew he could be, even he had no idea how to say what he needed to say next.

Luckily Maggie came to his rescue. "Darryl, JJ is suddenly very concerned that Lucas—being a painter and all—might be the arsonist." She put up her hand as she saw Darryl was opening her mouth. "I know what you are going to say—that the mere idea is crazy. I told JJ the very same thing myself. I told him how close Lucas was to Marilyn, and that we simply can't go around accusing every painter we meet of arson, and that there was a very good chance you were going to stop allowing Penny to see him again if you got wind of this new obsession of his. Yet he has remained concerned. That said, I'm happy to see JJ showing the initiative to come talk to you about this matter in a mature way. So I suggested we come speak to you directly."

Darryl seemed winded by this speech. "Ask me what, exactly?" She turned to look at JJ. "Ask me if my brother is a murderer?"

JJ shifted uncomfortably in his seat. "Not exactly. Ask you if he has a tattoo of a paintbrush under his cast."

Darryl seemed to relax considerably. She shook her head in amazement. "JJ, I have never, your entire life, known what to make of you. You were very precocious as a child, did you know that? Always up to something and always ready with an explanation." JJ thought that was a little harsh—his dad had always said he was curious, not precocious—but he didn't say anything. "Then, after the fire, you were so very angry... I was certain there was no hope for your emotional recovery. Now here you sit, calmly asking me, with no evidence whatsoever, if my brother is an arsonist." She stood up and cleared her throat. "Jacob Jasper Jones, I am happy to report to you that my brother does not have, and never has had, any tattoos."

Maggie stood as well. "Thank you, Darryl. I'm sorry for the intrusion on your time." She nodded jerkily to JJ, and he pulled himself up from the couch quickly.

"Yeah—I mean, yes." JJ stood as well. "Thanks, Darryl. I'm sorry if I made you upset." He paused. "Sorry for being, you know, hard to figure out too, I guess."

"Well, JJ, it is something you could work on," Darryl practically barked as she led them down the hallway. On that note, she slammed the door behind them.

Maggie sighed and ran her hands through her hair. "I truly hate to say it… but I think that went well."

JJ didn't answer.

By the time they got home, the spring had wound so tightly JJ was sure it was going to break.

He sat on his top bunk, rocking himself back and forth, thinking about the party Lewis had invited him to that night. He almost rocked himself clean off the bunk before he finally reached for the pamphlet Dr. Ben had given him.

Inside was a list of twelve things teenagers who had a problem with alcohol did—stuff like "guzzling" what they were drinking or letting their grades slip. Next to almost every item on the list was a picture of a teenager looking either depressed or hopeless.

Well, except one picture of some kids dancing together at a party. JJ couldn't help but think that it looked like they were having a pretty good time.

The pamphlet said that if even one item on the list applied to you, you might have a problem with alcohol.

And there were only three that *didn't* apply to JJ.

A few hours later, JJ was ready to do what he needed to. He reached for his cell phone.

JJ: Come over?

McKinley didn't answer right away. It was almost ten minutes before JJ's phone buzzed.

McKinley: Y

It was a legit question, so JJ answered it.

JJ: Need to talk to u.

There were another few long minutes before McKinley answered.

McKinley: b there soon

About half an hour later, JJ heard Maggie answering the door. He was listening to "Separator" by Radiohead—one of his, and McKinley's, favorite songs. Maggie knocked on JJ's door.

"McKinley's here to see you, kid," she said, poking her head into the room.

Thom York was singing about whether or not something was really over as McKinley walked in and closed the door quietly behind him.

McKinley smiled. "Good song," he said quietly.

That was all JJ needed to hear. He took a pamphlet off his dresser. "I need to go to this AA meeting," he said, showing what he was holding to McKinley. "I called them. I guess Moreville's too small to have meetings just for teenagers, but they said teenagers go to the regular meetings here. That it's no big deal. And I don't want to go alone."

The smooth chords of the guitar filled the room around them, and JJ thought it felt like they were lighting up the space between him and McKinley. Thom York went on about whether or not he was waking up from a dream.

McKinley nodded. "Yeah? Where'd this come from?"

JJ hesitated. "I thought I found him. I thought it was Lucas, McKinley. I thought I finally found him. And everyone says I'm wrong, and I had to talk to Darryl. And it isn't him." JJ cleared his throat. "It didn't work, the benefit, and then I thought for sure it was Lucas, but Darryl says he never had a tattoo. I realized I might never know who Tattoo Man is, you know?"

McKinley nodded again.

"I didn't drink yet, though. I really wanted to. I, uh, still do. I took the pamphlet test instead. And then I texted you."

McKinley smiled, and the spring began to unwind just a little bit. "Of course I'll go with you, JJ."

Thom York begged to be woken up. It really was a great song.

CHAPTER 11

THERE WAS no doubt in JJ's mind that he was getting seriously paranoid.

As Lucas picked Maggie up for what would be their third date, and JJ sat in the kitchen listening to them chuckle and giggle at each other, he couldn't help but admit that Lucas was nothing but a gentleman to his aunt. He held coats, doors, chairs, and everything else a guy had to hold in order to be considered chivalrous. He was witty and told a lot of quick jokes that made Maggie giggle. JJ knew from overhearing Maggie on the phone that she was really into Lucas.

And Darryl had said he'd never had a tattoo on his hand. So why was JJ still convinced he couldn't trust the guy?

Maggie returned from the hallway to tug her keys off the countertop. "JJ, we're just grabbing dinner. You can feed yourself, yes?"

JJ nodded and waited numbly while she kissed him on the forehead and swept out of the kitchen.

He watched out the window as Lucas opened the car door for Maggie like the perfect gentleman that he was.

No doubt about it, JJ thought as he grabbed his coat and ski hat and left to meet McKinley. He was getting paranoid.

McKinley led JJ into the room at the hospital where the AA meetings were held. This was only JJ's second, and JJ hadn't been very proud of his performance at the first one. He'd managed to get out that his name was JJ and that he drank a lot, but that was about it. Still,

McKinley had told JJ he thought JJ had done really well. "Rome wasn't built in a day, JJ," he said, as JJ sulked on their ride home. "You went. You said who you were. You admitted to having a problem. That's, like, awesome."

And at least it turned out that the "anonymous" part of Alcoholics Anonymous was pretty legit. JJ recognized at least one person from his school there, a senior, and neither of them had even acknowledged each other since the meeting. So that was good.

The person running this meeting did the introductory statement, and together they recited the same weird thing they'd recited last time: "Grant me the strength to accept the things I cannot change, courage to change the things I can, and wisdom to know the difference." At first, JJ had thought it was really strange to start a meeting with group chanting. It made the whole thing feel a little cultlike. But then he thought about what the saying actually meant, and he decided that he kind of liked it. And that it wasn't a bad way to open a meeting with a bunch of people who were on track to drink themselves to death.

JJ listened as one of the older guys in the group talked about how his wife wanted to leave him, and he didn't know what to tell her, and how it was hard to know when to give up on something and when not to.

Then another person talked about losing their parents.

Then someone else talked about losing their son.

"Can I say something?"

JJ's voice was so quiet that he almost couldn't hear it.

"Of course, JJ." The person who had led them in the chant smiled encouragingly at him.

"I wrote a poem." He pulled the paper from his pocket. "Uh, I don't like talking about this stuff. Or myself. But this is my second meeting, and I haven't had anything to drink in a while, so I think maybe I'm ready. I like writing poetry lately, so can I share that way?"

"Of course, JJ."

"Great. It's called 'Unbreakable Cycles.' It's actually a revised version of a poem I wrote a while ago." He couldn't help but glance sideways at McKinley when he said that.

Unbreakable Cycles

Sticks and stones, they told me
Break bones, they told me
Words, they told me
Don't hurt, they told me

The words have come
Always, with fire behind them
The fire of bad news,
And anger,
And problems

I have responded to these words
With a fire of my own
Fire that brings more words
Of bad news,
Of anger,
Of problems

But I am trying
To move away from the fire
And you keep coming with me
And your words are the right ones
And sometimes you make
Unbreakable cycles seem breakable

The group started clapping, and JJ let out the breath he hadn't realized he was holding.

"I NEVER realized just how stupid-boring Moreville is."

JJ had to laugh at that. They were in the library a week later, once again scouring the newspapers from the weeks after the fire, looking for any other little clues they could find—and it was true, their town was dead boring. JJ was pretty sure he'd lose his mind if he had to read one more piece about a bake sale or a grandson who came *all the way from New Hampshire* to visit their grandparents. Barf.

"Huh." JJ clicked on an icon for a headline from the local paper that he'd never noticed before.

CLOTHING STORE OWNER MOVES ON AFTER LOSING HER PARTNER

MOREVILLE—These days, Darryl Lane knows a few things about fighting grief by keeping busy. As she balances a baby on her hip while waiting on a customer at her used clothing store, Second Time Around, one can't help but think that she could use some help around the place.

One would be distressed to know that Lane had plenty of help just a month ago—until she lost both her business partner and best friend to the Bijou Street Movie Theater fire.

Lane, along with Marilyn Jones, has owned Second Time Around for almost four years. The business has thrived in the small community of Moreville, where people always seem eager to sell old clothes as they buy used ones. Three weeks ago, the staff of Second Time Around was rocked when it learned that Jones, along with her husband, Jacob, had been in the Bijou Theater during the fire and had not survived.

"I'm still in shock," Lane says about learning the news. "Marilyn and I have known each other for well over fifteen years. We went to school together. Opening this store was a culminating moment in both of our lives. We were so proud of it; so proud of each other. I still can't believe she's gone."

Lane celebrates the life of her lost best friend in many ways, particularly through her children. Lane currently has custody of Jones's young daughter, Penny, the baby she often brings to work with her these days. Lane has already vowed to adopt Penny and raise her alongside her two sons. Jones's son Jacob, age five, was badly burned in the Bijou fire and is currently recovering in Moreville General. Darryl is planning to adopt him as well.

"We know it will be a long road for JJ," she says of his recovery. "He witnessed some terrible things that day. I'm confident my family can become the support he needs right now."

As for keeping the store open during such a difficult time? "I never even considered closing it," Lane says with a slight smile. "I know how much it means to Marilyn that I keep it open. For her."

JJ gagged a little, but he forced himself to examine the picture at the bottom again. There were four people in it. JJ easily recognized three of them. One was dating his aunt right now. One was a younger, but no less menacing-looking, Darryl. The last face he knew held the beautiful and soft smile he remembered so well: his mother's. One was a stranger.

He focused his blurring eyes on the caption below: *The staff of Second Time Around, together at a party two weeks ago. From left, Darryl Lane, Lucas O'Dell, Marnie Sanfras, and Marilyn Jones.*

Marnie Sanfras? Who was that? JJ had certainly never heard of her. Of course, he'd never heard of Lucas O'Dell until two weeks ago.

"Hey, McKinley? Do you think this woman is worth checking out?" JJ pushed the ledger over to McKinley and tapped the picture.

McKinley read the caption. "Interesting. She worked with your mom and Lucas?"

"Yeah. I still don't trust him. I'm probably just crazy and paranoid, I know. Darryl said herself Lucas doesn't have a tattoo."

McKinley considered that. "Still, there's something about him that bugs you. Maybe it's even just that he knew your mom and you didn't know him. Talking to this Marnie woman—about Lucas or your mom—might help somehow. Maybe."

"Maybe." JJ shrugged again. "How am I supposed to find her, though? I mean, I doubt she still lives here."

McKinley scoffed. "JJ, we've just spent the last three hours realizing how tiny-ass our town is, and you're worried we won't be able to find this chick?" He shook his head. "So much for me thinking you were some amaze-balls detective. We'll go ask my mom." He pushed back the hard-backed library chair and stood up, stretching. "She knows everyone in this town."

JJ fidgeted. "Uh, sure. Go for it. Call me and tell me what you find out?"

McKinley laughed. "Oh no. You think you're getting out of it that easily? You're coming too, Buster. Why are you so afraid of my parents, anyway?"

"Not afraid," JJ mumbled. No, a nervous wreck was more like it. McKinley's parents were just so... nice. So put together, always smiling at JJ and offering him cold drinks. JJ spent every moment he was around them certain that at any moment they'd realize he was an ex-alcoholic screwup who was corrupting their son and ship him out of their home. "I have a lot of homework," he whined.

"Nope." McKinley shook his head. "We do this detective thing together, JJ. Let's go."

"Fine," JJ grumbled. "But can we stop off at the hospital on the way there? I have to pick up the schedule for my community service next week."

"I thought you finished your hours."

"I did. But they still need people. So I offered to stay on."

McKinley's eyes widened. "Jacob Jasper Jones, if I wasn't worried that you'd completely flip out if I did it in public, I'd stick my tongue down your throat right now."

That made JJ laugh... and silently thank McKinley for not doing it. He might be coming to terms with liking guys, but he wasn't ready to tell the world about it the way McKinley did.

McKinley came into the hospital with him and waited patiently while one of the nurses found JJ's schedule. "Thanks for staying on with us, JJ," she told him. "We're really short people right now."

"Yeah," said JJ. He told her good-bye and nearly ran right into Jeremy when he turned around.

"JJ," Jeremy nodded. "Nice to see you. Who's this?"

"This is McKinley," JJ told him. "McKinley, this is Jeremy, one of the physical therapists here. McKinley, is uh… my boyfriend."

It was the first time he'd ever used the words, and he was surprised to hear them come out of his mouth.

McKinley nudged him. "Dude, I appreciate you actually getting the words out, but it will be a lot nicer to hear when you don't sound like you're being tortured into saying them."

Jeremy barked out a laugh, and JJ looked at him in surprise. The entire time he'd been working there, he had never even heard Jeremy chuckle.

Jeremy caught his glance and shrugged. "I remember those days." He shook his head. "You guys have… fun. Have a fun day." He walked off, and McKinley and JJ headed to McKinley's house to keep "working the case," as McKinley liked to say.

Sure enough, McKinley's mother knew who they were talking about. She told them that she had gone to school with Marnie's sister, and she was pretty sure Marnie still lived on Willow Street in the house with the cow mailbox. Then she insisted JJ stay for dinner, and he spent the whole time terrified he was going to spill spaghetti sauce all over her tablecloth, and McKinley spent the whole time "accidentally" brushing him on the knee, trying to make exactly that happen.

But there were plenty of good parts about the evening. Like the fact that no matter how nervous JJ got, he didn't want a drink once the entire night. Not with McKinley sitting there next to him, smiling sideways at him in between bites.

CALLING WOULD have been easier, JJ thought, as he looked up miserably at the large gaping green house in front of them. It was the Saturday morning after they'd found the article. Snow had been coming down hard all night, and JJ had been planning to sleep in, but McKinley wasn't having any of that. "We know where she lives," he had told JJ the night before as he insisted that they meet at 9:00 a.m. "We need to get on this clue right away."

JJ had looked at him incredulously. "You're not Alex Cross, you know," he'd said.

"Who's Alex Cross?" McKinley had asked.

JJ shuffled his way up the stairs and toward the doorbell. All night long he'd been rehearsing what he might say to this woman he'd never even heard of, this woman who supposedly knew his mother. And he still wasn't sure what he was going to say.

"Hello?" The woman who answered the door was a little younger than his mom would have been, maybe in her thirties. She was mousy-looking, with brown hair and a sort of slumped expression, but she was definitely the woman from the photo.

When a few moments of silence made it clear that JJ wasn't going to be saying anything anytime soon, McKinley finally spoke. "Hello, Ma'am. I'm McKinley, and this is JJ. We're here because we heard you used to work at Second Time Around."

The woman's face suddenly rewrote itself with surprise, recognition, and regret. "Marilyn's son," she whispered.

JJ wasn't surprised when they were invited in.

"I had heard that Darryl adopted both you and Penny," Mrs. Sanfras said, pouring soda into cups for both McKinley and JJ as they sat in her living room. "But you said you're living with your aunt?"

"Yeah." JJ shrugged. "I tried living with Darryl, but we didn't get on too well. She did adopt Pen, though, Mrs. Sanfras."

She snorted. "Call me Marnie. And that woman's an ice queen. I hope she's treating Penny better than she treats every other person on the planet. You're lucky to have escaped her grasp, JJ."

JJ decided he liked Marnie Sanfras.

"Darryl is... well, you know what she can be like. It was your mother who hired me, you know, and I adored her. I was fresh out of college, back living with my parents, and I couldn't seem to find a job as a teacher, which was what I really wanted to do. Working for your mother was nice in the interim. She loved Darryl, and insisted to me that I just never got to see the kinder side of her. And I swear to this day that I never did. That woman showed me almost no respect. After the fire, I quit that job within a month."

"Why didn't Darryl like you?" McKinley asked, reaching for another cookie.

"I suspect it started when I couldn't get along with her brother, Lucas. He was in college, taking courses at UVM, and your mother and Darryl hired him on part-time. Man was a pain. Did nothing but moon after your mother all day. Of course, she was a saint about it—always kind when she put him off, never complained to Darryl. Still, I thought it was obnoxious, and I wasn't shy about saying something to him. He hated me after that."

JJ almost spit out his soda. "*Mooning?* You mean... he had a crush on Mom? She was married! With two kids!"

"Yes, yes, I know. He did, too. Lord knows your father dropped by often enough to visit. But the boy was obsessed. He followed her everywhere, picked up extra shifts when she'd be working. Marnie's eyes suddenly grew sad. "She *was an amazing* woman, JJ, I'll give Lucas that. I'm sorry you didn't get to know her better."

JJ kept his gaze on his soda. "Yeah. Me too."

He'd forgotten what he was going to say next, but he was saved by McKinley. "Listen, you don't know if Lucas had any tattoos, do you, Mrs. Sanfras?"

"Tattoos?"

"Yeah." Now JJ stepped in. "It's kind of why we're here. See, I've been having this dream, and I'm pretty sure it's of the arsonist. And in it, he has this tattoo of a paintbrush. I met Lucas for the first time recently, and he has a cast covering his whole hand, so I can't tell if he does or not. And my aunt says it's crazy to think someone like Lucas would do something like that, but...."

Mrs. Sanfras frowned. "Are you asking if he could be the arsonist, JJ? I don't think so." She set down her drink. "I never thought Lucas was right in the head, JJ. Chasing after your mother the way he did, some of the strange things he said." She frowned. "When he and I did have a disagreement, or whenever he became upset, he would do especially strange things. Pace the store talking to himself. Very odd.

Still, do I think he could do such a thing to all those innocent people?" She shook her head. "That's much harder to believe.

"I can tell you that I never saw such a tattoo on his hand. However, his right hand and wrist were bandaged in the days just before the fire. When I asked him what happened, he refused to tell me. He just said he'd had an accident."

McKinley cleared his throat. "You mean... bandaged up like they do after someone gets a tattoo?"

Mrs. Sanfras seemed to be carefully keeping her voice even. "Yes, I suppose. Yes indeed."

All three of them were silent for a moment.

"JJ," Mrs. Sanfras finally said, "I suppose it's admirable, this desire you have to find the person who wronged your family. Still, I feel I should add here that it is highly unlikely Lucas is the culprit. Yes, I've always thought some counseling would be good for him, and yes, I can't say for certain he did not get a tattoo before the fire. But I can confirm that Lucas cared very deeply for your mother. It's hard to imagine him doing anything to harm her." JJ nodded. What she was saying made sense. So why was this meeting only further convincing him that Lucas was the arsonist? Mrs. Sanfras smiled and patted his hand. "You know, I've requested to have Penny in my class next year."

"You teach at Penny's school?"

"I sure do. I was hoping to have you as a student as well, but you ended up at the other elementary school in Moreville, didn't you?"

JJ nodded. "You should probably be glad. All my teachers hate me."

McKinley shook his head. "Not true," he said. "Our creative writing teacher loves him."

"That makes sense." Mrs. Sanfras stood and took JJ's face in her hands. "You have your mother's intensity, but you also have your father's face. And your father, you know, was a poet."

"What?" JJ had never heard that before.

"Well, more of a songwriter, I suppose. He had a small band; they often played in bars around here. He wrote all the lyrics."

JJ was floored. Maggie had never mentioned anything about this. "Why didn't I know that?"

"The band stopped playing after you were born. Jasper was obsessed with being a good father—insisted on putting you and Penny first. He always said he'd take up playing again when you were a little older."

"My father was a singer? And he wrote the songs?" JJ whispered.

"He certainly did. JJ, I would have liked very much to have had you as a student." Mrs. Sanfras winked. "I like a good challenge, you know."

THE WEEK after the visit to Mrs. Sanfras wasn't a great one for JJ's grades. His mind was definitely anywhere but his schoolwork. It was on Lucas, and theaters, and tattoos, and cycles, and sometimes on McKinley, but definitely not on geometrical equations or writing history essays.

And it wasn't a great time for that kind of thinking, because the semester was almost over, and midterms were coming.

A quiz in English class proved that JJ's recent successes might not even show up in his final semester grades: D+. His teacher smiled apologetically as she handed out papers to the students exiting her class, and she said something about how he'd been on the right track and he shouldn't let a slip like this get him down. He ignored her, snarled at the paper in his hand, and went off to find Lewis. He needed a drink. Then he remembered he didn't drink anymore, and he went off to find McKinley instead.

Only McKinley was in class, like the good student that he was, and he was ignoring JJ's texts—because good students never answered text messages in class. But Lewis wasn't a good student, and he eagerly met up with JJ at the bathroom on the second floor.

Lewis was stoked that JJ had texted him. "Let's get out of here and go do something. I was worried you were getting *boring*; we haven't partied in, like, forever," he told JJ as they snuck out a back door of the school. JJ had never told Lewis that he'd joined AA, so he just shrugged.

A few blocks away from the high school was an older, abandoned building that had once been an elementary school. It still had an old swing set next to it, and JJ knew from experience that it was a decent place to get away to during the afternoon without anyone else noticing. Most of the people who lived in that area were at work during the day, and Lewis's house was on the way there. Which made it easy to stop and grab a bottle of tequila from his father's liquor cabinet.

At the park, Lewis drank, and JJ stared at the bottle when Lewis offered it to him. "Uh... maybe I shouldn't." JJ stood up and paced around in front of the swing set. McKinley would be so pissed. But McKinley wasn't around, either, and that stupid spring had itself completely wound up over that D+.

Lewis snorted. "Should've known. You've been a total pussy lately."

"Screw you." JJ grabbed the bottle.

Lewis laughed. "It's true. Lately all you want to do is hang out with that fag. And at least he used to be cool, but he doesn't party anymore either. It's like he turned you gay and you two decided to be nuns or something." He cackled hysterically at that. "Gay nuns! Get it?"

JJ's spring coiled even more tightly. "What the fuck did you call McKinley?"

Lewis shrugged. "He's a fag. I mean, it's not like he hides it or anything. And he's okay, I guess, but he's definitely a fag, I bet he takes it up the butt and everything—"

JJ punched him in the eye.

"Asshole!" Lewis grabbed his face. "What's wrong with you, man?"

"I'm a fag too!" And then JJ knew why they called it "falling off the wagon," because it really *felt* like he was falling off something when he tipped the bottle back and the first drop of tequila hit his throat. He guzzled for several long moments before he ripped the bottle away from his mouth and yelled "And I don't care if you know anymore!"

Lewis just sat there, holding his face in one hand, his mouth half-open. JJ wasn't sure if he was even sober enough to comprehend what JJ had just said. Lewis looked like he might be about to say something when JJ's phone beeped, reminding him that he was due at the hospital for community service.

"Shit! It's already 3:30?"

Now he was going to have to go to work buzzed. Oh well. Who cared? The afternoon was proving that there really wasn't any hope for him, no matter how many sappy poems he wrote.

LUCKILY JJ hadn't had too much of the tequila, so no one at the hospital seemed to notice right away that he was swaying once in a while and hadn't been able to properly hang up two clipboards.

Until he ended up standing next to Jeremy at the nurse's station.

Jeremy was filling out some paperwork when he started sniffing the air around him. JJ felt his neck going a little red.

"What's wrong with you?" Jeremy asked quietly.

JJ squinted up at him. "Huh?"

Jeremy shook his head, anger filling up his features. "You may be able to fool everyone else with Altoids, but not me. Your eyes are totally unfocused, and I can smell the liquor behind the spearmint. How dare you to come work at this hospital drunk?"

The next thing JJ knew, Jeremy was hauling him to his feet and dragging him away, calling out to JJ's supervisor that he needed to borrow JJ for a moment.

"Where are you taking me?" JJ hissed.

Jeremy didn't answer, but the button he pressed once he'd hauled JJ into the elevator made it perfectly clear: Dr. Ben.

JJ wrestled out of his grasp. "Just get me fired, okay? Who cares? Tell my supervisor. I don't have to be here, so who gives a shit?"

"Oh no, you don't." Jeremy crossed his arms and glared at JJ. "I know you talked Ben into getting you this gig, and all he talks about lately is you. He thinks you're some great kid who's trying to get his life turned around and do better. Well, you're going to look him in the eye and tell him exactly what you did today."

JJ's eyes watered.

Jeremy dragged JJ unceremoniously into Dr. Ben's office, where JJ wound his hands together and tried not to throw up the tequila sitting in his stomach. He felt like he was back in the police station, waiting for Maggie to pick him up.

He thought he'd come so far since then. Maybe some cycles really were unbreakable.

Dr. Ben opened the door to the office. "Jeremy? Did you page me here? What's going on?" He saw JJ standing there. "JJ, is everything okay?"

When JJ didn't speak, Jeremy growled, "He came to work drunk."

Ben scowled. "JJ? Is this true? Are you drunk?" Ben came to stand directly in front of him and sniffed. "I'm calling your aunt," he said, shaking his head. "JJ, how could you do this?"

And then the tears felt like they really were about to come, and Dr. Ben was looking at him just like Maggie had that day at the police station, and just like McKinley was going to look at him when he found out, 'cause there was no way he wasn't going to, and like his parents would be if they were still alive, and the worst part of all was that JJ actually *cared* that Dr. Ben was looking at him like that and that Maggie and McKinley would be too pretty soon. Which really sucked, because JJ was sure he'd been right before: he couldn't break the cycle himself; his only hope was to catch the arsonist. But he hadn't been able to prove Lucas was the arsonist, and he probably never would figure out who had killed his parents, and the cycle was just going to keep going and going and going. He couldn't stop it. But he could go back to not caring.

"Fuck that," JJ told Dr. Ben and Jeremy. "I'm outta here." He started for the door.

"Like hell you are," Dr. Ben snapped. "You're not going *anywhere* alone like this. Stay with him, Jeremy," he added, and then left the room, cell phone in hand.

JJ dragged himself to the couch in the office and sank into it. He thought briefly about trying to fight Jeremy to get out of the room, but that seemed a little dramatic, even for him.

It didn't seem like it had been nearly long enough when Maggie came charging into the office with Dr. Ben behind her.

"JJ? What did you do?" Anger was practically radiating from her features. "Dr. Ben says you came to work... drunk? Is this true?"

JJ didn't answer.

Dr. Ben sat down next to JJ. "JJ, does your aunt know everything that's been going on with you?"

"Some of it," JJ mumbled.

Maggie's eyes widened at that. "What's been going on, JJ?" she asked.

JJ knew he'd been keeping a lot from Maggie, and he wasn't even sure why. After all, she'd listened when he'd needed her to listen—gotten him a fast court date when he'd needed it to see Penny again, helped him ask Darryl if Lucas had the tattoo. Not to mention all the years before that when she'd stuck by him no matter how many bad school conferences and angry door slams she'd had to put up with. She'd given up so much for him.

JJ thought that might actually be why he hadn't said anything about the other stuff, like going into AA and dating McKinley. Even though Maggie had proven time and time again that she would stay loyal to JJ, the idea of disappointing her even more than he already had turned JJ's stomach.

Maybe it just wasn't possible to not care about someone when all they did was care about you.

All three of them were *looking* at him—staring, even. Maggie sank onto the other side of JJ on the couch, so it was like she and Dr. Ben had JJ surrounded, and Jeremy was standing across the room, watching the whole scene with a face so still that JJ had no idea what he could be thinking.

And maybe that tequila hadn't totally worn off, because suddenly JJ was crying. A lot. And talking.

He was talking about drinking too much, and being with McKinley, and deciding to go to AA, and about finding Marnie Sanfras, and what she had told JJ and McKinley. "And then I got that D+ today," JJ finished up. "I found Lewis. We went to the park. He had tequila… and he called McKinley a fag. I told him I was too." He finished up the whole speech with his eyes on Maggie, thinking she—and maybe Dr. Ben too—would finally have to throw in the towel now, because how could any person possibly handle all that?

Maggie just wrapped her arms around him, though. "Oh, sweetheart," she whispered. "I am so sorry you've been carrying this around. I wish you'd said something." She kissed his forehead. "JJ, I want you to be able to tell me anything. Just like you would have been able to tell your parents anything."

"Even all this?" JJ whispered. "Even that I like guys?"

"Yes, JJ," she said, squeezing his hand. "I am one hundred percent positive that they would have loved you no matter what."

"Even that I'm in AA?"

"Especially that, JJ. Only I don't think that would have happened if they'd been here." She shook her head. "I've done a horrible job with you, JJ. I've let you down so badly."

"No!" JJ was horrified. "Don't say that, Mags! Don't ever say that! I'm the one who let you down!"

Then they were both crying, and it didn't seem to matter much who had let who down.

JJ had almost forgotten Dr. Ben and Jeremy were still in the room at that point, but Dr. Ben reminded him when he patted JJ's shoulder and said, "So you joined AA?"

"Kind of." JJ smiled wryly. "I mean, I don't have a sponsor right now or anything. I just go to the meetings. But I guess McKinley was kind of like my sponsor." JJ's face fell as he thought about telling McKinley what he'd done that afternoon.

"And you told your friend you're gay. JJ, that's very impressive."

"After I punched him," JJ admitted. JJ heard a strange sound from the other side of him and realized that, for the second time, he was hearing Jeremy laugh.

"And you still believe Lucas could be the arsonist?" JJ was startled when Dr. Ben quietly asked the question.

JJ sighed. "Probably not, I guess." He snuck a glance in Maggie's direction. "But I just can't seem to stop thinking that he could be."

After a long moment of silence, Jeremy said, "I have to get back to work." But before he left the room, he said, "Don't come to work smashed again, and I'll make sure no one finds out about this."

Dr. Ben stood up and stretched. "You know, JJ, I think we should stop and acknowledge something pretty impressive here: the fact that you came to work at all. After all, people make mistakes." He locked eyes on the door Jeremy had just closed. "No one's perfect, JJ," he muttered.

ON THE way home, JJ told Maggie a little more about his conversation with Mrs. Sanfras.

"Mrs. Sanfras told McKinley and me that Lucas was in love with Mom. And that he was a little… messed up then. Are you sure he's not the arsonist, Maggie? Like, absolutely sure?" JJ asked.

"Yes," Maggie said fervently. "But you're not, and I want to value what you think. He gets his cast off soon, right before Christmas. I promise that if there is anything remotely strange about that process or how his hand looks afterward, I'll look into this further with you."

JJ nodded. "Okay. I guess I can live with that. I mean, Christmas is coming up pretty quickly."

Maggie's expression dipped. "Actually, I've been a little worried lately that he won't even be here that long. He said he's having a hard time getting any shows up here, and he'll need to go back to his studio in Boston if he can't find something soon."

JJ was surprised by just how sad she sounded. He'd been too busy being preoccupied with how dangerous Lucas could be to even think about him just straight up breaking Maggie's heart. "Uh, sorry, Aunt Mags," he said. But he could only worry about Maggie for a minute before his thoughts went back to the fire. What if Lucas left before JJ got to see his hand without the cast?

Maggie shrugged. "It is what it is. He needs to work, and his buyers are in Boston." She chuckled. "Just not enough rich folk around here, you know?"

But it occurred to JJ that he knew at least one rich person in Moreville. And she was just bored enough that she might be willing to do something ridiculous like put on an art show so JJ could see a hand.

It was a win-win idea, as far as JJ was concerned. If Lucas's hand did have the paintbrush, then JJ could finally break the cycle. And if it didn't? Well, at least, Maggie could stay happier a little longer.

CHAPTER 12

MCKINLEY: Where were u after school? U texted earlier?

The text came in just after dinner. JJ was pacing his room, trying to work up the courage to text McKinley back.

JJ: Home
McKinley: U skip last period?
JJ: Maybe.
McKinley: Knew u wer trouble

If only he knew.

JJ: sorry
McKinley: u okay?
JJ: have to tell you something
McKinley: ?
JJ: I messed up
McKinley:?
JJ: I got a D+
McKinley: Too bad. :) U will do better next time

JJ: Pissed me off

McKinley: That y you texted

JJ: yeah, you were in class tho

McKinley: sorry about that

JJ: I went to the park with Lewis

McKinley: WTF, JJ?

JJ: i know

McKinley: kid is bad news

JJ: i know

McKinley: next time wait for me ok

JJ: i had tequila

JJ: i'm really sorry

JJ: like really really

JJ: he called you a fag. i told him about me

JJ: u there?

But McKinley didn't answer.

JJ kept pacing, hoping desperately that the phone would buzz back. The spring was tighter than ever, but JJ was determined not to give in to it and go looking for alcohol. He wasn't sure he'd be able to get any, anyway. If Lewis had told everyone in their group about what had happened at the park, there wasn't going to be anyone left to party with.

He circled the room, wheels turning. McKinley was gone. JJ had finally managed to ruin that. But Dr. Ben didn't think he was a total lost cause, and Maggie still loved him. That had to be worth something, right?

He just needed something else to do. Something else to think about. So he decided he might as well put his next plan in motion.

He wasn't totally truthful with Mrs. Somersville. He *did* tell her that he'd stolen her number from his aunt's phone. He was just a little less honest about the reason *why.*

"See, Mrs. Somersville, my aunt has started dating this guy, a painter. And she really likes him a lot. But he's leaving, I guess because he can't seem to get a show around here and he was doing pretty well where he used to live, in Boston and that area. So now he's saying he needs to go back soon. I was thinking, though, that if you could help get him a show around here, maybe he'd stay awhile? At least through Christmas?"

Mrs. Somersville was laughing halfway through JJ's well-rehearsed speech. "Well, aren't you a little matchmaker!"

"I just want my aunt to be happy."

JJ didn't feel too badly saying that, because it was at least half-true. If it turned out Lucas didn't have the tattoo, JJ would be very happy to see him and Maggie live happily ever after.

"Well, shows can be hard to come by, darling. But I do have lots of time on my hands these days, and a few friends...."

JJ grinned triumphantly. He *was* going to see Lucas's hand.

When he clicked off the phone call and realized McKinley still hadn't texted him back, JJ spent the next hour repeating that over and over in his head.

HE KNEW the wheels had been set in motion when Maggie came bustling into the house for dinner a few days later with Lucas on her heels. "JJ, we have wonderful news!"

JJ was cooking spaghetti. "Yeah?" He nodded at Lucas. Lucas didn't spend much time at their house—he and Maggie usually went out, which JJ assumed was because Maggie knew how uncomfortable Lucas made JJ. Still, when Lucas and JJ did come in contact, JJ did his best to be as cordial as possible. JJ assumed Maggie and Darryl had never said anything to Lucas about JJ's suspicions, because Lucas never acted strangely around JJ.

"Lucas finally got a show! And you'll never guess who set it up!"

JJ tried hard to look confused. "Who?"

"Do you remember that woman we met at the memorial that night? Mrs. Somersville? The one who was trying to set up more social events in this area? Well, it turns out she heard Lucas was in town, and she remembered his work from when she was living in Boston, and she got one of her friends who owns a local restaurant to agree to show Lucas's work there over Christmas!" She clapped her hands. "Isn't that *wonderful?*"

JJ drained the pasta and pulled a grin onto his face. "That's great, man. I guess that means you're hanging around, then?"

"Yes, it does. At least until the New Year." Lucas's smile stretched a bit. "I am excited to get to spend more time with your aunt."

Maggie blushed red with excitement. "It's going to be a great holiday this year, JJ. Not just you and me! Darryl's invited us all over to her place for Christmas, and the show opens the day before Christmas Eve.

"That's great, Aunt Mags." JJ went for the hug she was offering.

"So, Lucas," JJ asked nonchalantly, "that means you'll be able to get the cast off and get some painting done here, right?"

Did a shadow cross Lucas's face, or did JJ imagine that? He couldn't be sure.

"Yes, JJ, it does," Lucas said. "Right before the show."

And that was how JJ began counting down the days not until December 25, but until December 23.

MIDTERMS WERE a lot easier when you actually studied for them. It was the twenty-second, the last day of school before break, and JJ just needed to get through this last school day to get to zero hour. Seeing Lucas With His Cast Off Day was what he'd been calling it in his head.

First Day Without Fucking School might have also been appropriate. School had been rough ever since the tequila incident. McKinley hadn't even glanced JJ's way in over two weeks. JJ texted him for a while, trying to get a response, but McKinley never texted back. JJ tried a few times to work up the nerve to go talk to McKinley in the halls, but one look at the crowd of friends that surrounded him always had JJ backing off. It was clear that McKinley was really pissed, and JJ wasn't sure McKinley wouldn't put him in his place right in front of a crowd of people.

Lewis had been really weird around JJ ever since that day. He never said anything about what JJ had told him in the park, and he and JJ still ate with the same crowd at lunch, but Lewis was constantly looking at JJ oddly—like there was something about JJ that he was trying to figure out. It had started making JJ so uncomfortable that he'd actually eaten lunch in the library a few times.

Yeah, a break from school was definitely going to be welcome.

At least Creative Writing didn't have a midterm. All JJ had to do to get through that class was write and listen to some workshopping.

"Writing time first today," Mrs. Lyle told them. "Then we'll move into our final workshops of the semester." She pulled up the day's writing prompt on the projector at the front of the class. "Revise a piece you've been working on throughout the semester. Choose one that you feel is still unfinished, or one that you worry still isn't right somehow."

The class got to work, and JJ stared at the screen for a while.

Then he started writing.

He wasn't quite finished when Mrs. Lyle called time, but he was close enough. He didn't even hesitate when she asked for the first volunteers of the day—just raised his hand.

To her credit, Mrs. Lyle called on him as if he raised his hand every day.

JJ swallowed hard before he began speaking. "This is that poem I workshopped for you guys a while ago. I've revised it a few times since then. Maybe now it's finally finished." He let his gaze pass over McKinley, but McKinley was staring down at his desk. "But I kind of don't want it to be finished yet," JJ added. And then he started reading.

Unbreakable Cycles

Sticks and stones, they told me
Break Bones, they told me
Words, they told me
Don't hurt, they told me

The words have come
Always, with fire behind them
The fire of bad news
And anger,
And problems

I have responded to these words
With a fire of my own
Fire that brings more words
Of bad news,
Of anger,
Of problems

But I am trying
To move away from the fire
Your words moved me farther
Than anyone else's ever have
They were the right ones
Honest, hopeful
They gave me hope,
And new honesty

And even if your words are permanently gone
Know that
You made this cycle seem breakable
And if I break it, it will be
Because of you

And I will always be sorry
I couldn't break it for you

JJ finished reading, and the class stared at him. Finally, Danielle Fitzpatrick raised her hand. "JJ, that was, like, awesome. Like, the most honest thing anyone in this class has ever said." She squinted at him slightly. "Sometimes it's like a poem is trying to hide what it's really saying, you know? And your first version of this poem did that a little bit, I think. But this one didn't feel that way at all." There were murmurs of agreement.

They critiqued him. They told him what they loved about it, and how he could still make it better. They studied it together. They didn't ask him details; they just helped him improve the writing. It would have been a great workshop.

Except that McKinley just sat there, looking at everyone except JJ, and never said a word.

BY THE time school ended, JJ'd never been so glad to hear a bell ring. He'd been checking his phone every five minutes, just to see if McKinley would text him. Nothing. The spring wound a few times, but JJ unwound it by reminding himself that he'd written that poem for himself as much as McKinley, and that he would be okay if things with McKinley were really over. At least now he would know.

He packed up his backpack and slammed his locker closed—and saw McKinley standing on the other side of it.

"Where are you headed?" McKinley asked.

"I have a shift at the hospital," JJ told him.

"Let me give you a ride."

When they were almost to the hospital and McKinley still hadn't said anything, JJ finally did. "You never texted me back."

"Yeah." McKinley focused on the road. "I know."

"I really am sorry."

"I know that too. Are you going to meetings again?"

"Uh-huh. I've been to a couple." One had been just a few days ago. "And I haven't had a drink since that tequila. I really am doing better. I just… made a mistake."

"I know. Listen, JJ…." McKinley paused for a few moments, and JJ tugged at his backpack threads while he waited. "It was crappy of me not to text you back. I was just so, like, *done*, I guess. I'd spent all that time trying to help you find Tattoo Man and stop drinking, and I knew I was the first guy you liked and all, and that's a lot of pressure too. Then you just went off with Lewis the first time things got really hard, and I thought that I didn't want to deal with it. Didn't want to be the person always trying to fix you or something."

"I guess I get that." So they really were breaking up, for good this time. JJ hoped he wouldn't cry during his shift. Jeremy was going to start thinking JJ was a total wuss.

"Then you read the revised poem today." JJ perked up a little when McKinley said that. "And I remembered that I've been really lucky, JJ. You were right when you said I had a great life. Not perfect, but really great. I figured out that I was gay when I was pretty young, and people have been mostly supportive, and I've never lost anyone I really care about, or had to fight for the people I love, or gone through half the shit you've gone through. When you were reading your piece today, I remembered how strong and amazing you really are—to go through all that and still come through a human being on the other side? It's amazing. You're amazing."

He pulled up into the hospital parking lot and turned to look at JJ. "I'm sorry I bailed when things got tough."

"Me too," said JJ.

"I know. I should've known that right away. I like you so much, Jacob Jasper Jones."

And then instead of crying, JJ was making out with McKinley in the middle of the hospital parking lot where anyone could see them.

"I wanna tell people," he told McKinley when they finally pulled away. "I wanna go to the next GSA meeting with you and tell people you're my boyfriend. Who cares? Plus, people should be fine. The universe owes me some luck, right?"

McKinley laughed and hugged him, and this was definitely the best Last Day Before Christmas Break ever.

As JJ pulled on a scrub top and got ready to start his shift at the hospital, he thought about how he couldn't remember the last time he'd been this happy. Things were so good: he had McKinley back, he was spending Christmas with Penny, he'd come clean with Maggie, and he had Dr. Ben now too. He hadn't had anything to drink in weeks, and his grades were going to be okay this marking period.

He wondered if he needed to see a tattoo on Lucas's hand the next day to stay this happy.

"Hello, JJ."

JJ looked up to find Jeremy standing next to him.

Jeremy sniffed the air. "Glad to see you're walking a straight line today."

JJ rolled his eyes. "Ha ha. Thank you, by the way. For bringing me to Dr. Ben instead of just getting me fired."

Jeremy snorted and began sorting through files in front of him. "I should have had you fired. I just knew Ben would say you were worth another chance."

JJ thought about that for a few seconds.

"That's because I am," JJ finally told him, just loudly enough that he was sure Jeremy could hear. "I think maybe everyone is."

CHAPTER 13

THE ART show was being held at La Vida, a small Italian eatery just a few doors down from the Bijou. It wasn't as formal as the benefit had been, and JJ was happy Maggie let him wear his polo shirt and some khakis she'd gotten ahold of and ironed. As they walked past the theater to the restaurant, Maggie reached for JJ's shoulder and grabbed him in a tight half hug.

"JJ, I really am proud of how far you've come over these past few months."

They were almost to the restaurant, and JJ didn't want to make a scene around all the people who were going to be there, but he had to ask. "Do you think Dad would be proud?"

Maggie whirled JJ around to face her. "JJ," she said softly, "wherever he is, your dad *will always* be proud of you."

JJ shook his head. "It's nice of you to say, Aunt Mags, but we both know it isn't true. He wouldn't have been proud of me a few months ago. But I think maybe I'm getting there. Thanks for waiting all this time. Thanks for... being there."

She squeezed him in a tight hug, and it was all JJ could do to get her to let go of his hand before they walked into the restaurant.

Half of the restaurant had been transformed into a gallery, and was covered with paintings, large and small, that dotted the walls. Waiters scampered around with trays of food, and JJ snagged something that looked, but did not taste, like a pig in a blanket. Then he started walking around.

Most of the paintings were abstract, if JJ was remembering his ninth-grade art class correctly. To him, they just looked like shapes that were put together in weird patterns with weird colors. They were pretty enough, maybe, but he caught a look at one of the price tags, and he sure couldn't imagine paying that much for a bunch of colored shapes.

He walked around, trying to figure out what some of the paintings were, and then he saw it: the one painting in the entire exhibit that JJ understood perfectly.

The top of it was large triangles of orange aiming for a large head of curly hair, and then JJ knew that Lucas probably *had* been in love with his mother, at least at one point, because that was her head. Even if the face was just a mix of circles and squares, that was his mother. JJ was sure of it. But it was what was below this representation of his mother that JJ understood even better.

It was another head, a drooping oval, and teardrop-shaped pieces of black leaked from it. Surrounding the bottom of the head were the orange triangles, and they stretched back into the distance of the canvas.

JJ had been wrong all along.

He was no big art fan, and he could never have explained to anyone why that painting proved to him, once and for all, that Lucas was innocent. It was just something in the way that the painting was exactly how *he* felt about that fire. And about his mother.

JJ didn't need to see Lucas's hand to know that he wasn't Tattoo Man. The proof was right there on the wall.

He just stood there for a moment, frozen, staring at the painting. Around him, people kept moving, talking about it. "It's called "Every Inferno," someone whispered quietly. "What an interesting title."

Then JJ spotted Lucas over in the corner, chatting with Mrs. Somersville and another woman he didn't recognize. She was hiding Lucas's right arm from view.

Taking a deep breath, he tried to look as casual as possible as he headed over to them. "Hello," he said.

"JJ!" Mrs. Somersville shook his hand excitedly. "I was just chatting with your aunt's... *friend.* He's so talented! I'm so glad we were able to make sure this show happened!"

JJ waited, tapping a toe anxiously, while both women gushed over Lucas's incredible talent. And he studied Lucas's hand.

The cast was gone. But his right hand, peeking out from the sleeve of his suit jacket, was covered in the kind of bandage you used to wrap a sprain.

When the women finally saw someone come in that they *had* to go say hello to, JJ found himself alone with Lucas.

"What's wrong with your hand now? You got your cast off."

Lucas glanced down. "It's just been sore. The doctor suggested I use this when it's aching."

JJ kept his gaze on Lucas. "You don't have a tattoo under there, do you?" he asked, even though it didn't sound much like a question to him.

For a minute JJ thought Lucas was going to make a snarky remark or laugh at JJ. Instead, he asked, "Why? What tattoo do you think you'll see on my hand?"

JJ considered the question. "One I already know isn't there," he finally said.

Lucas pulled down the wrapping on his hand just a notch, just a few centimeters. Just enough that JJ could see... a birthmark.

"What were you looking for, JJ?" Lucas asked quietly.

Well, JJ thought, no sense in holding back. Not at this point in the game. "I thought you did it. I thought you set the fire, all those years ago."

Lucas looked incredulous. "Me? You thought *I* set that fire? You thought I killed your parents and all those people?"

"Well... yeah."

"*Why?*"

"Lucas, darling, come meet my friends!" Darryl called from across the room, interrupting the conversation that JJ quickly remembered wasn't all that private.

JJ studied his feet, and Lucas grabbed his shoulder. "Don't go anywhere after the show, okay? We need to talk, you and I."

McKinley arrived an hour later. "Sorry I'm so late. I was trying to get out of the house earlier, but Dad's relatives are all visiting for Christmas, and my Aunt Lisa just never stops *talking*." He rolled his eyes. "My mom told them all about you, by the way. They can't wait to meet you."

Great.

"So what happened? Did you see his hand yet?"

JJ nodded. "It isn't him. That thing I thought I saw under the cast? It was a birthmark. Not a tattoo of a paintbrush."

McKinley frowned. "Are you sure? You don't think he could have had the tattoo removed or anything?"

JJ glanced over at "Every Inferno," which a whole group of people was standing in front of now. "Yeah. I'm sure. I told him what I'd thought, though. He says he wants to talk after the show."

"Are you going to?"

JJ shrugged. "Sure. Why not? What do I have to lose?"

They sat in seats by the bar and watched people walk through the makeshift gallery. "Wow," McKinley sighed. "I really thought it could be him. What do we do now?"

JJ frowned. "Yeah. I don't know. I mean, what did we do before? Hold a benefit to draw the guy out of hiding. Well, if it did, we didn't catch him. What's left? It was ten years ago. I can keep looking for that tattoo on every arm I see. I may never find it." He sighed. "I have to face it, McKinley. I might never know who Tattoo Man is. I might never know who killed my parents. No matter what I do, I might never be able to break this stupid cycle I'm stuck in."

"JJ, think about that poem you wrote. You *are* breaking the cycle. You really are. You don't need to find this guy to do that."

JJ wished he could believe that.

McKinley grabbed his hand then, and JJ was proud that even though half the town could see them, he didn't even think about pulling away.

The show ended, and JJ and McKinley helped Lucas and Maggie clean up a bit and load some paintings into the back of Lucas's SUV. Then Lucas asked Maggie if it would be all right if he took JJ home.

Maggie looked intrigued, but all she said was "of course."

McKinley left, Maggie told them that she was going to meet some friends for drinks, and then JJ was in Lucas's SUV.

They were barely out of the parking space before Lucas brought up the topic of the fire. "You really thought I was the arsonist, huh?"

"There were clues," JJ said mildly. "I mean, you are a painter, and the fire was started with turpentine. You disappeared for years after the fire, and you were pretty vague about why. You had that cast, and I know the arsonist had a tattoo of a paintbrush on that part of his hand."

"How do you know that?" Lucas wanted to know, and JJ filled him in on the dream.

"And there you were," JJ finished up, "with that exact part of your arm covered."

Lucas seemed to consider that. "I guess that makes sense and all," he said. "But *why* would you think I would do something like that? What kind of motive would you think I would have?"

JJ shrugged. It was time to throw poor Mrs. Sanfras under the bus. "So, I met this woman who used to work with you and Mom. She was telling me all kinds of things about how you used to be in love with Mom—like obsessed. I didn't really know what that might mean, but she made it sound like it was, I dunno, stalkerish or something. I guess I started to think maybe you killed her because you couldn't have her."

"Ahh… you talked to Marnie." Lucas nodded.

JJ was startled. "You mean it's true? You really were like that with Mom?"

"When I met your mom," Lucas said quietly, "I was kind of a mess. Darryl doesn't like to admit it, but the real reason she hired me to work at the store while I was starting college was because I couldn't get hired anywhere else. I have some… mental issues, and I wasn't in counseling then, and I was kind of all over the place.

"Your mom, though, never cared. She never treated me like I was different, or off, or not okay. She just... helped. She always helped. So I fell madly in love with her.

"I did resent your dad, and you and Penny, for existing. I desperately wanted to be a bigger part of her life."

Well, *that* was a little awkward to hear from someone you'd just crawled into a dark car with, even if you had just convinced yourself they were Not a Bad Guy. "Are you still like that?" JJ asked. "In love with her?"

"No." Lucas shook his head. "After the fire, I realized how unhealthy my feelings towards your mom really were. I did go back to counseling. I will forever miss your mother," he added. "Sometimes terribly. But for the right reasons now, I like to think. Because she was an amazing, life-changing woman who was there for me when nobody else was. And I certainly don't resent you anymore, JJ," he added.

That was good to hear.

"What about the bandages?" JJ asked. "Marnie said you had bandages on your right hand right before the fire. I thought maybe that was because you'd gotten a tattoo."

Lucas groaned. "If I tell you what really happened, JJ, will you promise you won't hold it against me? I haven't told your aunt about this yet, but I do plan to."

"I guess," JJ said hesitantly.

"I told you I was having a rough time of things then. I... attempted to take my own life."

"Wow," JJ said. "Just... wow."

"Yes. It was a terrible time for me. But it led to some good things. I ended up finally getting some counseling, which was what I needed."

Neither of them said anything for a few minutes. "What about Aunt Mags?" JJ finally asked. "Are you gonna leave?"

"I don't want to," Lucas said. "But Maggie and I both know that we don't have much of a possibility for a future. National Geographic has been offering your aunt her gig back whenever she wants it, so the second you go off to college, we'd be toast anyway."

"Whoa." JJ's eyes widened. "My aunt could get her job back anytime?"

"Pretty much. They think she has incredible untapped potential. I mean, it's not as if they wanted her to leave in the first place."

Huh. That was interesting.

"Yup. So we don't really have a future, anyway. No matter how much I might think of her."

They reached JJ's driveway, and he climbed out of the car. "Thanks for bringing me home," JJ said.

"Of course," said Lucas. "And JJ, I'm sorry you've spent the past few weeks probably terrified as hell whenever I was with your aunt. You could have talked to me. I would have gotten the cast taken off just to show you what was really there."

JJ shrugged. "Then I probably would have just convinced myself you had the tattoo removed or something." He shook his head. "I needed to figure it out on my own, ya know?"

Lucas nodded slowly. "Yeah. I get that, JJ."

JJ figured he probably did.

CHAPTER 14

IT WAS a good thing Christmas was only two days later. JJ's dream was back in full force, and he hadn't slept through a night since the art show. But when Penny answered the door at Darryl's house, squealing as soon as she saw her aunt and brother on the other side, JJ forgot all about that.

"JJ! We get to spend Christmas together!"

JJ grabbed Penny up in a bear hug, thinking that statement was long overdue.

David clapped him on the back and said it was great to see him again, and he and Dennis had some pretty decent conversations about the colleges Dennis was applying to. Lucas and Maggie spent most of the day holding hands, occasionally looking at each other all googly-eyed. When everyone opened presents, Penny insisted on curling up next to JJ the entire time. It might have been one of the best days of JJ's life.

Until Patrick decided to ruin it.

Dinner was over, and JJ was sitting in the living room, waiting for Penny to get some art project that she wanted to show him. Patrick stepped into the room and practically growled when he saw JJ. "Are you still here? Don't you have some other family you can go bug?"

JJ felt the spring start to coil. "Grow up, Patrick. Penny is my family. And why are you always such an asshole, anyway? It's not like you still have a reason to be pissed off at me."

"Oh yeah?" Patrick charged toward JJ then, and JJ stood up quickly. "You don't remember what you did to me, Jones?" He pointed to a tiny scar on his left ear. "You sent me to the fucking hospital! You gave me this for life!" He shook his head. "At least Ma had the good sense to kick your ass out after that. But you just keep coming around."

JJ set down the soda he was holding. "Yeah? You want us to keep being pissed off about this? You want this to keep going? Well, here's the thing, Patrick. If most people in this house right now knew what you said to me that day, I'm pretty sure you're the one who wouldn't come out looking so good. And right now I'm not sure why I've spent all these years not telling them."

"Whatever," Patrick said. "Like they'd believe you anyway."

JJ smiled. "Hey, Dennis!" he called. "Come in here a minute."

"Dennis won't believe you," Patrick said, but JJ heard a hint of uncertainty in his voice.

"Oh God," Dennis groaned as he walked into the room. "Are you two going at it again?"

"Maybe," said JJ. "But first, Dennis, did Patrick ever tell you what we were fighting about that night your mom kicked me out of the house?"

Dennis looked back and forth between them. "He said you got mad because he took a toy from you or something?" His eyes stopped on Patrick. "That not true, Pat?"

"It's true," Patrick said hastily.

"No, it's not," said JJ. And cycles and art shows and dreams may have been a little too fresh in his head when he said, "Patrick told me that God wanted my parents to die, and that's why he had someone set the theater on fire. Patrick told me that my parents must have done something pretty horrible for God to punish them like that."

Dennis's face was white. "Pat, is that true?"

Patrick seemed to put great effort into rolling his eyes. "Maybe I said something like that. But I was six, dude! I didn't mean it. I was just pissed off that Mom and Dad kept paying so much attention to JJ. It was like you and I didn't even exist anymore. Plus, we had that weird church school teacher that year, remember? The one who was always talking about God punishing sinners? I just repeated what she kept saying all the time. It didn't give JJ the right to beat the crap out of me."

Dennis shook his head. "JJ was six too. And yeah, I think it kind of did give him the right. JJ, why didn't you ever say anything? Maybe if Ma knew that was why you guys fought, she would have let you stay."

JJ shrugged. "Patrick didn't say anything, so neither did I. I always said I wouldn't tell until he did."

"You are one stubborn shit, JJ," Dennis told him. "Patrick, I can't believe you. You just let JJ get kicked out after that?"

"He beat me up!" Patrick cried.

"Whatever. You know I'm telling Ma about this, right?"

"I don't care," Patrick mumbled, but JJ saw his body slump as he said it.

"You know what? Don't," JJ said.

"Excuse me?" Dennis responded as he and Patrick turned to look at JJ at the same time.

"Your mom and I are finally getting along, and I get to see Penny almost as much as I want right now. And it's Christmas. So let's just have Christmas. And maybe Patrick here can stop growling every time I walk into a room in your house, and we'll call it even."

Dennis looked surprised, but all he said was "Patrick?"

Patrick crossed his arms. "I'll try, I guess."

Then Penny came running back in with her art project, and it really was an excellent day. The only downside was that McKinley was spending it with his family.

Even that was okay, though, because JJ went over to his place after the celebrations at Darryl's were finished.

JJ thought he did okay not making a total ass out of himself in front of McKinley's relatives. After the meeting-the-family obligations were out of the way, he and McKinley sat next to each other on the floor against McKinley's bed, listening to some album McKinley had found called *Alternative X-Mas.* It was pretty good. Especially R.E.M.'s "Deck the Halls."

"I'm glad you got to spend Christmas with Penny this year," McKinley said.

JJ smiled into his hot chocolate. "It was awesome. First time I've felt really good on Christmas Day in years."

"Can I ask you a question?"

"You mean there's one left you haven't asked me?"

"Eff you. Seriously, can I?"

JJ was pretty proud that he could say, "Of course."

"Everyone says you refuse to dress out for gym class. Why?"

JJ listened for a moment to the music swirling around him and considered that. He leaned into McKinley. "I have all these scars all over the backs of my legs," he said. "I don't want people to see 'em, you know? And I don't want to wear sweatpants, because then people will start asking all kinds of questions that I won't want to answer."

McKinley just nodded at that and rested his head on top of JJ's for a second. "Thanks for telling me," he finally said.

"Now I get to ask you a question," JJ said. "How the hell did you know about my Finch stories?"

"Oh… that." McKinley grinned. "Mrs. Lyle isn't the greatest at keeping secrets. She let it slip one day when we were talking after class. Said she thought you were going to be a great novelist one day. That made me want to get to know you better… so when you showed up at the library that day and needed my help, I had the perfect opportunity."

"Blackmailer."

"Proud of it, too."

It was another few long minutes before McKinley said, "Merry Christmas, JJ."

A broad grin spread across JJ's face. "Merry Christmas, McKinley."

That evening was the first time JJ let anyone see all of his scars.

THREE NIGHTS later, JJ closed the door and watched McKinley back out of the driveway before he started the short walk up to his house. The AA meeting had been good. He was going to get a sponsor soon, which he was looking forward to. It would be nice to have someone to bug besides McKinley whenever the spring started to coil and JJ started to feel twitchy. And then he and McKinley had gone to a movie where a bunch of people had blown crap up for two hours. Overall, a good night.

JJ reached his front porch and saw something strange: a note pinned to his door. It was strange for a few reasons. For one, Maggie always just texted him when she needed to get a message to him. For another, Maggie had been gone all day photographing a wedding in Burlington, and she shouldn't have been home yet.

JJ pulled the note from the door.

JJ-

Come to the graveyard behind the Methodist Church. Come alone if you want to know who set the Bijou fire. DO NOT CALL THE POLICE OR TELL ANYONE WHERE YOU'RE GOING or you'll never know.

-A friend

JJ scanned the dark yard around him, not surprised when he didn't see anyone there. It was after nine o'clock, which meant the majority of his sleepy neighborhood was dark.

McKinley's car was already gone, and JJ was grateful for that.

He stared at the note for a minute, and he thought about cycles, and Maggie and McKinley, and Dr. Ben asking him how much his own life was worth.

And then he thought about the dream, and the faceless man who still kept appearing, night after night.

He turned and started walking toward the graveyard.

THE METHODIST church wasn't far, and within twenty minutes JJ was standing under the lights from the back of the churchyard, wishing he'd brought a flashlight. And a hat. A cold December wind had picked up and was swirling snow off the ground and around the spot where JJ stood.

The gate to the graveyard was locked, and JJ wasn't sure what he should do about that. Wait for someone? Jump the fence? It was a small fence, that was for sure. It wouldn't be hard for anyone to jump.

JJ was studying the gate, trying to figure out if there was some way to open it and wishing again that he'd had the foresight to bring a flashlight, when a voice behind him said, "Don't scream." Then JJ felt something hard and metallic press against his temple.

Odds were pretty good that it was a gun.

"WHO ARE you?" Those were the first words JJ was able to get out of his mouth, and they felt pretty strangled. In his defense, he'd just been forced at gunpoint to hop a fence and march through a graveyard. Anybody in that position probably would sound a *little* strange.

"That's not important," the gun owner said. But it sounded like a woman.

"Oh. Um, where are you taking me?" In the near-complete darkness of the graveyard, it was hard to see where the gun owner, who was holding his right arm, was directing him. And it was a little strange that she seemed to know exactly where she was going, despite the fact that there was only a sliver of moonlight guiding them.

She stopped walking. "You'll find out right now," she told him, and brought him to a standstill in front of a grave.

She kept the gun trained on JJ as she moved around to stand in front of him, next to the grave. It was hard to make out her features in the dark, but JJ thought she looked almost tiny, short and without much weight on her. "I don't want to hurt you," she said in a low voice.

That seemed counterintuitive to her actions, but JJ didn't say anything.

"See, I heard you the other night," she told him. "At the restaurant. The art show. Talking to your friend. I heard you talking about the fire, and how you were looking for a man with a tattoo. I heard you say the benefit was your idea. You said you *needed* to catch the person who set the Bijou on fire. And I knew it was finally time to tell someone. I knew I was finally ready."

For the first time since that gun had pressed against JJ's skull, it wasn't the only thing he could think about. "It's you? You're the arsonist? But I thought it was... a man...."

She shook her head. "It wasn't me. It was my brother."

She gestured at the gravestone behind her, and JJ thought he probably would be sick. In the thick darkness he could barely make out the words ERIC POORCHESTER, 1985-2003.

"Did he die in the fire?" Now JJ was pretty sure his voice was actually *croaking.*

"Yeah," the gun owner whispered, taking her eyes off JJ momentarily to touch the gravestone, almost affectionately. "They found his remains in Theater Three."

Instantly JJ was suspicious. "How can you be sure he was the arsonist, then? Whoever set the fire in Theater Three left." That much he knew for sure.

She sighed and shook her head. "I didn't know for sure it was him, not right away. But eventually I figured it out. I paint, and all my turpentine went missing that day. I still don't know how he ended up back in Theater Three. In all the chaos, he must have gone back in to die there. But I do know, absolutely, without a doubt, that Eric set that fire."

The gun shook a little in her hand, but JJ knew he was going to ask his next question no matter what that gun did.

"Do you know why?"

She kept the gun trained on JJ as she spoke. "Our mother had been killed in a barn fire a few years earlier. She was a hired hand at a farm up the road from our place. The owners were trying to get the insurance money for burning it down, and she got caught in the blaze. The owner only got twenty years in prison." She paused. "He's out now. Good behavior.

"So I knew he was angry, because Eric was always very angry. But I never knew he was capable of something like *that.* Then the fire happened, and I wondered. Then I realized my turpentine was missing, and I *knew.*"

The gun was still there, but JJ couldn't stop himself from asking, "Why didn't you ever say anything? You could have saved so many people so much pain."

She shook her head again, and the gun shook along with it. "Don't you understand? I thought *you* would understand! The man who set the barn fire. His wife went to the movies that day. *She was at the movies.*" Even in the deep darkness around him, JJ thought he could see her eyes water. "And Eric was still my brother. I couldn't tell anyone. I couldn't let anyone know what he'd become."

She made a strangled sound before she went on. "I don't know what went wrong for him, exactly," she said. "Or why it went wrong for him and not me. But I know that there are some people you love so much that you protect them even when you shouldn't. You believe in them even when you shouldn't."

JJ saw Maggie in his mind's eye. And Dr. Ben.

"You know," JJ said slowly, "You didn't have to get a gun to bring me out here and talk to me. All you had to do was tell me you knew who set that fire. You can put that down."

"No." She shook her head rapidly. "Then there would have been police, and news reporters, and other people, and I wouldn't be able to do what I need to do at the end of this." She did something to the gun, making it click loudly, and JJ realized that Dr. Ben had been right: no matter how much JJ had wanted to know what happened to his parents, finding the answer wasn't going to be worth dying. Not with McKinley ready to go to more AA meetings with him. Not with Penny excited to read with him at the library next week. Not with Maggie and Dr. Ben believing in him even when they shouldn't.

JJ wished he'd realized earlier just how right Dr. Ben was. "Why me?" JJ demanded. "Why just me? There were so many people in the theater that day."

"Because you *cared*, JJ. Because you cared enough to hold a whole party looking for the person who did this to your family. And because of what you said in that restaurant. You said something about how you could never break the cycle. That's what convinced me it was time for this. I knew then what I had to do." She shook her head. "JJ, the cycle has to stop. It has to end. You have to end it."

JJ closed his eyes and tried to think about how at least he'd be seeing his parents again soon. "Will you at least tell me your name?" he asked.

There was a strangled laugh. "I suppose it doesn't matter anymore, does it? Cara," she told him. "My name is Cara."

"Cara," said JJ. "Cara, you're not really going to do this, are you?"

"I have to," he heard her say. "But first, there's one thing you should know. That tattoo you were talking about. I don't know how you know Eric had a tattoo on his hand, but he did. Only it wasn't a paintbrush. It was our mother's name: Louise."

"Louise," whispered JJ.

"Louise. He wasn't a bad person, JJ. It's just that the world shit all over him, you know?"

"The world shits all over a lot of people," JJ replied coldly, opening his eyes again to make sure Cara was listening when he said that. "All kinds of people." Then he remembered something Maggie had said to him once. "You can't ride on the coattails of your pain your whole life."

Cara touched the gravestone again briefly. "I don't think you have that right," she said. "It's not that you *can't* ride on the coattails of your pain your whole life. It's that you *shouldn't*." And before JJ could say or do anything else, Cara turned the gun and pointed it squarely at her own temple.

And pulled the trigger.

JJ WAS huddled in blankets in the police station when he finally saw Maggie. She rushed toward him and JJ tried to stand up, but his knees wouldn't hold him. She grabbed him when he started to sink back onto the chair, and they sank down together, holding each other.

"Oh my God," Maggie kept saying. "Oh my God. Are you okay? I finally finish photographing the wedding from hell only to find a phone message from you about how something happened and you're in a graveyard and I shouldn't worry because you've already called the police and you're sure they'll be calling me soon and then I get a message from Detective Starrow saying you were held at gunpoint and they're taking you to the *police station* and I should meet you there? And *are you okay?*"

"He's fine, ma'am," Officer Favor said, walking over to them with Detective Starrow by his side. "Just shaken up." He smiled at JJ. "But if anyone can handle what he just went through, it's this kid."

JJ held on to Maggie. "Yeah," he said to the officer who had arrested him, all those months ago. "Yeah. I'm going to be fine."

Maggie shook her head. "What the hell happened, JJ?"

Detective Starrow gave a wry grin. "We've actually been waiting on you, ma'am, so he could give a full witness account with a guardian present." She patted JJ lightly on the shoulder. "And from what we've seen and heard so far, I have a feeling it's going to be one hell of a story."

JJ wasn't all that excited about telling the whole story again, especially when he got to the part about how he decided to go to the graveyard on his own without telling anyone. That earned him some *really* dark looks from two police officers and an aunt who JJ was pretty sure would soon be grounding him until the end of time. And that look was nothing compared to the one McKinley gave when JJ finally got to tell him the whole story the next morning.

"You almost got yourself killed," McKinley growled once JJ was finished.

"But I didn't." JJ frowned. "And I'm really glad, you know?"

McKinley nodded. "Good." Then his eyes widened. "Holy shit, JJ," McKinley whispered. "You know. You know who Tattoo Man was."

JJ shrugged. "I guess. I mean, it still doesn't make any sense, McKinley. Not really. I don't think it even made any sense to Cara. Not what her brother did, and not what she was doing. I said that to Maggie last night, and she just said it was never going to make sense, ever. Not any of it."

"I think she might be right," McKinley said. "But you're alive. That part makes sense."

Then they were kissing, and JJ knew that much, at least, was true.

CHAPTER 15

BIJOU THEATER FIRE CASE CLOSES

MOREVILLE—After nearly a decade, the long-standing mystery of the Bijou Theater Fire finally seems to have been solved—somewhat.

On Monday, police held a press conference to announce that they believe they have finally discovered the arsonist behind the fire. "The fire appears to have been set by Eric Poorchester of Trenton," Detective Jane Starrow announced at the conference. "Mr. Poorchester's sister came forward with information connecting Poorchester to the fire just before she took her own life."

Detective Starrow went on to explain that the motives for Poorchester's actions, however, were still not entirely clear. "We know Poorchester's own mother was killed in a barn fire set by an arsonist, and that the wife of that arsonist was at the Bijou the day Poorchester set the fire," Starrow stated. "However, why Poorchester chose to end the lives of so many is not entirely known."

Police have stressed that anyone with additional information regarding Poorchester should contact them immediately.

Dr. Ben dropped the newspaper next to his breakfast plate and shook his head. "Incredible. I can't believe that stupid plan you and your friend concocted actually worked."

"Hey!" JJ was indignant. "It wasn't that stupid. Anyway," he added, taking a bite of pancake, "it didn't really work. I mean, Eric Poorchester was already dead. He didn't come to the memorial."

"Yes, but Lucas might never have come back without that memorial... and then there might never have been an art show, and Cara Poorchester might never have overheard you and McKinley talking, and she might never have decided to tell anyone what she knew."

Or kill herself. JJ had spent a lot of time listening to people tell him that Cara likely would have taken her own life at some point soon whether or not she had overheard JJ.

He hoped someday he would believe them.

"What a crazy chain of events." Dr. Ben set aside the newspaper.

Fate, JJ thought. Or maybe just more signs from the universe. He still wasn't sure he believed in those, though. Dr. Ben shook his head again and signaled the nearest waiter for more coffee. "So. Not that I'm not enjoying our breakfast together, but I'm curious to know what you wanted to meet me at the diner for."

"Sure." JJ straightened up. "I have a... proposition for you."

Dr. Ben nodded and wiped his mouth. "Sounds serious."

"Kind of. I guess. I want to come live with you."

Dr. Ben nearly spit out a mouthful of egg. "Pardon?"

"Listen, I know it sounds crazy, but hear me out. My aunt's been putting off her career for me for years, doing what she thought was best for me. I don't want her to have to wait for me anymore. I want her to be able to go back to working for National Geographic. I heard her and Lucas talking the other night. They're getting pretty serious, and Lucas was saying that when she went back to work for NatGeo that he'd try to go with her, maybe to sell his paintings around the world or something." JJ paused. "I don't want her to have to wait anymore, you know? She deserves the chance to get that life back now. Anyway, I'm pretty sure you need me more than she does."

Dr. Ben looked bemused. "You think so, do you?"

"Yeah. You *get* it, Dr. Ben. You get me better than anybody, except McKinley. I think everybody should have that—someone who just gets them. Maggie has Lucas now. You had Jeremy... but I kind of get the feeling he didn't get it. That's why you guys aren't together anymore, isn't it?"

Dr. Ben studied JJ from across the table. "You are a very astute young man sometimes," he finally said quietly. "Particularly for someone with such trouble seeing what's right in front of you."

JJ snorted. "You should talk. You don't see how perfect this is? You're lonely. You have to be. You just spent Christmas alone, for crying out loud."

Dr. Ben frowned. "You really want to do this, JJ? You really want to try living with a hermit like me? Why? You could always ask Darryl, you know, if getting Maggie her old job back is really the big goal here."

"Over my dead body. Literally. Patrick and I would probably kill each other. Anyway, that's one goal here. But I also think it could be a goal that you and I help each other." He gestured to the paper. "This is bound to keep messing with my head in a big way once I wrap the stupid thing around it. And I bet it will mess with yours too."

Dr. Ben was silent for several moments before he spoke again. "I have two conditions."

"Shoot."

"You keep going to AA meetings."

"Sure. Easy. McKinley would kill me anyway if I stopped. But... I might slip up." JJ shrugged. "Nobody's perfect, you know."

Dr. Ben smiled.

"What's the second condition?"

"Well, it's a strange one. Jeremy and I may not be together anymore, but you've probably noticed that he's still very much in my life. I've gathered that the two of you don't get on perfectly. You'd have to be all right with Jeremy being around a fair amount."

That was easy. JJ thought of Jeremy on the day JJ had cried in Dr. Ben's office, and JJ was glad he'd figured out that things weren't always as black-and-white as he'd once thought they were. "No problem."

THREE MONTHS later, JJ spent his first night in Dr. Ben's house. He'd just come from an evening at the library with Penny and McKinley, and he was looking forward to hopefully finding an e-mail from Maggie and Lucas, who were traveling to the Middle East the next day.

He had a dream that night. But it wasn't the same dream he'd first had all those months ago. And it wasn't one of the dreams he'd been having since the graveyard—one of those weird convolutions of Cara and graves and guns.

It was a new dream.

A smell that wasn't there before suddenly filled the bathroom.

JJ drew in a deep breath, trying to match the scent to anything that might already exist in his short memory. It was a difficult scent to describe: like pine trees, but not the real ones in his backyard. More like the smell of the stuff his father used to get the kitchen floor clean.

He tried to push off the sudden sense of apprehension that filled him; who cared if someone else had also come into the bathroom? This was his town, the small town he had spent his entire five years in, and there was a good chance he knew whoever else had just joined him in the bathroom.

Even if he didn't know anyone who went around smelling like pine trees.

JJ took a few breaths and flushed the toilet, suddenly eager to get back to the movie and his parents.

As JJ shoved the door of the stall open, though, the scent grew weaker. When he finally wrenched the door wide and stepped out from the door, it was gone. The room was empty.

JJ woke up smiling.

Author's Note

IT'S NOT easy to write about a character who struggles with alcohol abuse. JJ was difficult to write at the best of times, and his issues with alcohol only made him more complicated.

The thing about alcohol abuse (especially where teens are concerned) is that it isn't always easy to understand. What's the difference between someone who just has a few sips of beer at a party and someone who's an alcoholic? Why do some people, and not others, end up abusing alcohol? How many teens who choose to drink end up abusing alcohol? There's a lot of confusing information out there on these topics.

According to a 2013 publication from the National Institute on Alcohol Abuse and Alcoholism, a 2009 study showed that 10.4 *million* people between ages 12 and 20 had consumed alcohol within the past month.[1]

10.4 million. That's a whole lot of young people.

So how *do* you tell if your friend is just having a few sips of beer at a party or if they're abusing alcohol? If you're concerned that either you or someone you know might have an alcohol abuse problem, go to the Alcoholics Anonymous website, http://www.aa.org, and check out their publication "A Message to Teenagers." Take the quiz there to learn more about what alcohol abuse really is.

And remember—even having a few sips of a beer at a party can be a big decision. JJ started his drinking with a few sips of beer at a party. Always be sure you're making the decisions that are right for *you.*

And if you or someone you know needs help overcoming a problem with alcohol, reach out to the following organizations for help.

---

[1] National Institute on Alcohol Abuse and Alcoholism, "Underage Drinking." Accessed March 18, 2014. http://www.niaaa.nih.gov/alcohol-health/special-populations-co-occurring-disorders/underage-drinking.

Alcoholics Anonymous
    http://www.aa.org
Teenage Addiction Anonymous
      http://www.teenaddictionanonymous.org/
The U.S. Department of Health and Human Services
Substance Abuse and Mental Health Hotline
    1-800-662-HELP

JOHANNA PARKHURST grew up on a small dairy farm in northern Vermont before relocating to the rocky mountains of Colorado. She spends her days helping teenagers learn to read and write and her evenings writing things she hopes they'll like to read. She strives to share stories of young adults who are as determined, passionate, and complex as the ones she shares classrooms with.

Johanna holds degrees from Albertus Magnus College and Teachers College, Columbia University. She loves traveling, hiking, skiing, watching football, and spending time with her incredibly supportive husband. You can contact her at johannawriteson@gmail.com or find her on Twitter at https://twitter.com/johannawriteson.

Also from JOHANNA PARKHURST

HERE'S TO YOU, ZEB PIKE

JOHANNA PARKHURST

http://www.harmonyinkpress.com

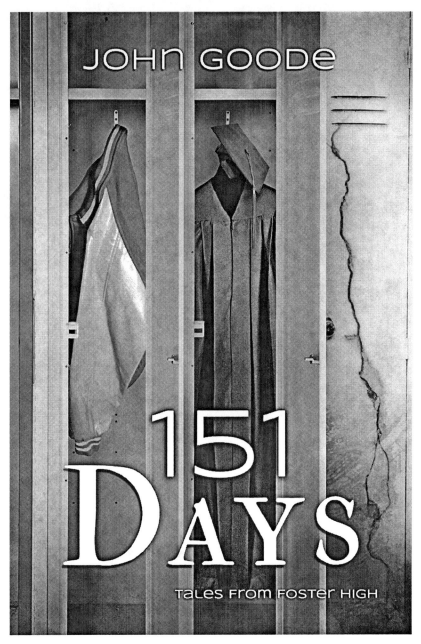

JOHN GOODE

151 DAYS

TALES FROM FOSTER HIGH

http://www.harmonyinkpress.com

Harmony Ink